RACE
~~CHASE~~ Between Law & Crime

Ashutosh Singh Rajput

Invincible Publishers

First published in India in 2017 by Invincible Publishers

ISBN: 978-93-86148-44-5

Invincible Publishers
G - 120, Sushant Lok III, Sector 57, Gurgaon-122002

Opposite Kasturba Ashram, Radaur Distt Yamuna Nagar, Haryana- 135133

Digitally Printed at Replika Press Pvt Ltd.

Acknowledgment

* * *

This first attempt has made me realize that writing a complete novel is not as easy as it seems. In this journey of several months, I would like to thank those special people who supported me and also who didn't, they also have an important contribution in the completion of this book.

First of all, the blessings of Amma and papa, grandmother and grandfather who are with us in every situation, whether they support externally or not. Apart from blessings, for the patience and support of Papa which I needed the most. My Amma, who is still in this confusion of what I am doing. My beloved sister's aspiration. Any amount of praise would be less for her. She also left no shortage of support.

My 'chhote Nana-Nani' have given the highest support as relatives. For my maternal uncle/friend Divyanshu and brother/friend Digvijay, who used to give me a positive outlook, where I get a glimpse of the heights I can achieve.

My close and humble mama/friend Vivek, who raised my courage against my expectations.

My most brave and distraught 'Sunita Mausi' who, without knowing the level of my talent, said that

I can not write the story, and my passion grew further after listening to it. Of course, after reading it, she will honor me with special ornaments.

All the friends whose first name and surname I have given to some characters of the story without telling them.

Ritesh, Ravish, Emmanuel, Yashwant, Anurag, Yogendra who always got excited whenever I would talk about my novel. They were always eager to know the release date

My publisher, Ajay Sir and his team, who completed the post-work and responded patiently to my questions.

My best friend Nikhil Tandon, who, while preparing this story, took my half of the burden. His help made my work very easy, without which it would have been very difficult to come so far. He has not only helped me mentally but was also ready for help financially. A true friend.

At the very end, that God has my belief that He exists everywhere and in everybody.

Preface

* * *

"There is no such a thing as coincidence. It is time that decides everyone's part and puts them together on its own way."

It is common or ordinary to give a lift when someone asks for that. But what if the person seeking for it is not a common man and what should happen when the person giving the lift is not ordinary. This perception has given rise to the basis of this story.

The story, filled with riddles, narrates about a man with extraordinary characteristics who is trapped in an extraordinary situations and later, his friends join and help him. Also, not to forget these extraordinary features come handy when they are used with intelligence and understanding. The whole story roams in Chhattisgarh state.

As One-Four-Three denotes few things in normal ways, just like that, It does the same instead of pointing just one particular thing in the whole story. In addition to one obvious reason, readers will be able to easily find out few reasons behind this name. The first few chapters of the story will definitely reveal the main issue of the story but this will only be an opening of the layers. The alternate events in the story will force the readers to go to other dimensions and put emphasis on intelligence.

The story deals with spice of fight, misunderstanding, conspiracy, mind tricks, love story and leaves the readers with the surprises.

Prologue

* * *

April 2014. Almost two years ago from today. A village in Uttar Pradesh.

A forest area surrounded by large and thick trees. It was 8 o' clock at night. There were some animal sounds. Homes were visible somewhere. Walls made of clay, grass and khappar were engaged instead of the roof. The area was too far from the city. The people here probably still did not know about luxuries like mobile or television. Or maybe they did but were not used to it. There are just a few original inhabitants living here.

"Is this 'that'?" A man holding a mobile in hand said. He had lit the torch of the mobile. Darkness had covered his face. Due to the light of mobile, thick mustache of his face was appearing. Eyes shining like light. Mobile's flashlight was focused in front of something.

"I think It is." Bowed down, the other person replied. On his hand was the same thing, which was to be the focus of the flashlight. He was also look-ing like a middle-aged person by appearance just like first one. That thing shining on his hand was looking like a stone. Because of the darkness, other man's face was not clearly visible either. Due to falling flashlight, a smile on his face showed clear. His eyes had the same sparkle like the eyes of the first one was. "Only this stone can glow in the dark like this." He said.

"Give me a cloth to cover it." He raised his hand and said.

The man behind the mobile flashlight gave him a small cloth. Here are three more people were standing behind these two. All of them appeared coeval. Their eyes were on that same thing. The last man behind them had also lit the torch of the mobile. They all were in an area situated near a mountain, looking down at the rocky ground. The village was not far away. There was very large sized stone around them. One was very close to them, the man had dug this stone there.

Covering that stone with the cloth, he stood up and turned to the man.

"Come on, let's go from here." He said. They all turned back and began to move forward.

They took a path from there. Five of these were in the urban ensemble. Of course, they were not native to the village. Moving forward, they passed the dense network of trees and reached the road. There was a car parked on the road. The man on forefront opened the door of the driving seat of the car. The other one from beside him had reached to the front seat. The other three were back at the door.

"Stop! You guys are making a mistake." They heard a hard and heavy voice. They turned back in respond to the voice.

An old man was standing in front. A flashlight was in his hand. In the name of the fabric, there was only orange dhoti and a sacred thread on the chest, long beard on the face and no hair on his head.

"Do not take this from here." He said.

"What are you saying, Baba?" Said the man standing beside the driver's seat.

"The stone is the angel of death. The stone has the dark history. Whoever comes in contact with it, dies." The old man's face was serious. Because of his deep voice and big eyes, his spoken words sounded even more terrible.

One of the spectacled man from among the people was standing at the back door, opened the door and said. "Do you even take the shits here. We have to leave early." He sat down on the seat, glided to the corner seat. The remaining two also sat next to him. Man standing in front of driving seat sat down on the seat. He rotated the key and started the car.

The old man quickly came to them and starts speaking fast. "You..You guys are making a mis-take. Taking the stone means starting...starting a row of death. All of you will get killed. No... no one can save you people...only a divine - eyed can stop the queue." The old man was kept saying but they ignored him and the car went forward. At last the old man shouted. "The prediction associated with stone never proved wrong."

The car goes away from him and he just stood there doing nothing, but see. In a few minutes, the car was out of sight.

Beyond Belief

* * *

A week ago from today. January 2016. Korba, Chhattisgarh.

"Wow! The restaurant is very beautiful Vivek! I had no idea about this place before." A beautiful girl said twisting her eyes around. Behind her was a young boy Vivek, pulling a chair to seat her.

"It just opened Sheena! I also didn't know." Said Vivek making Sheena comfortable and sitting opposite to her. Vivek's thick long hair seemed quite good on his slightly longer and wide face. Dark-skin colored face, healthy body and five feet eight inches tall, her personality was very attractive and impressive.

They were really happy with the restaurant. Entering in from the main door, different types of flowers mounted on the pots welcomed them with their fetching fragrance. After walking a few steps, a waiter came at the corner of the restaurant where their table was laid out. He greeted them with a smile. Such was the seating arrangement for the group of boys or girls who had come there in good number. Family or lovers added. Such was the seating arrangement that every table felt like the perfect spot in the restaurant.

Special lighting arrangements were on the tables for couples that made the place even more beautiful. Vivek and Sheena were sitting on one of these tables. This place was not very expensive either. Perhaps this was the reason that despite it was newly opened, it became much more customer friendly in less time.

Just as the waiter was approaching the two to take the order, Vivek signaled him to wait a while.

"Finally the 'Eid ka Chaand' came into view." Vivek said standing from his seat. There was a glow on his face.

"Vivek you? Here?" A young man of the same age or older than Vivek, with a beautiful girl was passing in front of him. Both of them looked at each other. He also enthusiastically came forward and shook hands with him.

"Yes! Had heard enough about this place. Thought of coming today." Vivek said. He pointed towards Sheena. "She is Sheena, my girlfriend." He smiled at Sheena. "Sheena! This is my school friend Nikhil Rathore. Police Force D.C.P." Sheena also smiled at him in response.

Nikhil called the girl standing behind him and said. "She is Payal, my girlfriend." Nikhil introduced Payal to Vivek and Sheena.

Deputy Commissioner of Police, Nikhil Rathore. Less than an inch small in stature and was a bit fairer as compared to Vivek. His shirt was sticking to his wide chest showcasing his healthy and muscular body. He was wearing glasses proving his weak eyesight.

The two were not very good friends. But they had a good rapport with each other. Nikhil and Payal went ahead just then Nikhil's mobile rang. After talking seriously in a low voice for a while, he came back to Vivek and Sheena.

Nikhil seemed a bit worried. "You three, get out of here." He said. "What happened? What's the matter?" Vivek asked.

Nikhil quickly informed him. "You had heard about a group of kidnappers of children in the news? They kill kids mercilessly if not provided with the money asked for."

"Yes! I heard." He said. Sheena and Payal had also given their ear towards them.

"The last incident happened two days ago right here. My 'khabri' just told me that they are right here in this restaurant. The government is holding very sturdy pressure on us. The worst thing is that we don't have their actual phiz. I have called the force. You three get out, there may be a risk here." Said Nikhil. The three listened to him and they got out of the restaurant.

Just while stepping out of the door, two police gypsy came and stood in front of them. The gypsy emptied and all the police force was standing and had taken positions. Here Vivek was busy protecting the two girls and hiring an auto for them.

"Why have called an auto? Aren't you going to drop us?" Sheena asked. She was surprised.

"No! You go. I have an important task to complete." Vivek made sure both of them were in an auto and came back to Nikhil.

After he arrived there, Vivek discovered that the four kidnappers were most likely there. But police not having their identity was a major trouble. Therefore, It was possible that among two hundred people, the kidnappers would escape. Nikhil and the police were in confusion.

"Nikhil! Come here." Vivek called Nikhil. "You are still here! I said..." "Can I help you?" Vivek said Nikhil interrupted in between.

"How?" Nikhil questioned. Vivek said by bringing him slightly away from others. "If you want them not to escape from under your nose, just do exactly as I say." He said firmly.

"But..." Nikhil hesitated. "Trust me." Vivek said and fixed his jacket.

Nikhil agreed. He told their partners to stay outside and be prepared. He and Vivek went inside again. Showing them his identity Nikhil told them that a thief was there who stole Vivek's purse. He told them to come to Vivek and to probe one by one.

Everyone present there took turns to come to him in the queue. Vivek was checking all men and boys. Vivek was checking them Just like the security man on the malls. Touching hands on the first upper pocket, then pockets of pants, front, and back. Men with families were let go without too much frisking. A group of four and five boys came to him. He let go of their investigations easily too. Then two groups of three boys and two boys came to them. He let them go by after their investigation. Vivek was frustrated and finally apologized to all and told them to go and sit.

"This was your plan? We have only wasted our time so long. After all, what were you trying to prove?" Nikhil flared upon Vivek.

Vivek manipulated his frustrated expressions

and told him smiling cleverly. "Was looking for a guilty straw, found. There are five of them, not four." Nikhil's eyebrows went up by listening to this. "What?" He said.

Ten minutes later the group of three and two boys passed from in front of them. They stared at Nikhil and Vivek and went out silently. They saw the gun in the hands of the police ready to move forward. Their expressions changed and they began to come back immediately after running. Nikhil halted his gun out and stopped them before they could join the others in the restaurant. They were unarmed. The police came and took them handcuffed.

Nikhil turned to Vivek after the matter was resolved. "Good Bye. Sheena would be waiting." Vivek said and tried to slide from there. "Wait!" Nikhil said in a strong voice.

"Shit!" Vivek's nose and eyebrows turned up, He closed his eyes and tried to think of a way to escape the situation.

Nikhil came to him and told him "Let's eat some food and you will tell me how you figured out their true identity without the police providing you with any information." There was a no choice for Vivek. His face was expressing his lack of desire to go. But Nikhil took with him.

Half an hour later.

Both were sitting at Nikhil's home. There was a table between the two, a wine bottle, two packets of chips and a glass was kept. Which was half empty. It was Vivek's peg. The second glass was in Nikhil's hand, which he had placed on the table. Nikhil, with his eyes tore and opened lips, was looking at Vivek. Vivek just told him how he identified the kidnappers. Vivek was expecting to hear something from his mouth.

"You're lying" The only words out of the mouth of Nikhil.

Chapter One

Two weirdos in a car

* * *

January 2016 . TODAY. Around 8 O'clock in the morning.

"Just gonna reach in an hour" Vivek said. He was talking on mobile with a Bluetooth headset in his ears. His hands were on the steering and eyes were looking straight on a secluded road. Few bikes and cars were accompanying him on this road. "How is your Dadu?" He asked.

"He's fine." Sheena's voice came from the other side of the mobile. "I'm sorry. I couldn't come with you to meet your parents." She said with a little sad voice.

"It's okay Sheena. But your visit was more important. I'll introduce you to my parents some other time. Where are you now?"

"Bilaspur! Will return tomorrow or the day after. Now put the phone down and pay attention to the road. Bye." Said Sheena. Vivek cut the call after replying 'bye'. The journey was quite long. He had, anyhow, passed one hour listening to the song and talking to his girlfriend.

Vivek was dying out of boredom and badly needed someone who could kill his boredom and entertain him while he could offer him lift in the journey. Vivek periodically caressed his hairs. Vivek at this time was heading for a town named Balco. Greenery could be seen all around the outskirts of the city. Peace and fragrance filled the air, making it more beautiful. After completing two kilometers of drive he saw some fuzzy thing on the road. A man had lifted up his thumb, which simply meant that he was in need of a lift. Vivek got a little excited as his wish was going to be true.

Vivek's car reached near the man who gradually appeared to look in proper shape. The man was standing. Behind him was a parked car which completely narrated the story. Its bonnet was open and exhaust gases from the radiator was still visible. Shaking his head, Vivek gestured him to come inside. The man opened the door and sat inside. A college bag on his back. He placed the bag on his lap and sat comfortably.

"Vivek Pratap." Vivek said forwarding his hand towards the man.

The man looked at his hand first and then saw him. "Raghav." He shook hands and responded in a very cold way.

Raghav's face was expressionless. The way of answering was matching his face. It seemed that he had barely laughed or smiled in his life. The fair skin had saved his face from being ugly. But hard on the face of the prospect of a short beard was slightly increased. Long hairs covering his neck and dark tinted aviators was definitely making him dreadful. Chilly winter morning had compelled him to wear a jacket, which was quite in accordance with Vivek's jacket. Those blue jeans was the only odd otherwise a black jacket over a black shirt was enough to call him 'man in black'.

For a while, they didn't converse and remained silent. Raghav was sitting with his flat face. Vivek again, looking in the rear view mirror, started caressing his hairs while he kept driving. The desire to overcome the boredom he had taken the initiative to talk.

"It seems to be less cold now?" He asked. Raghav did not respond to his questions. Vivek, for a moment, felt being a stupid. Raghav replied 'hmm' and he dropped the topic of discussion. Vivek got a little hint that Raghav is not interested in talking now.

Vivek stayed quiet for a while and suddenly had to ask again. "Well, what do you do?" He looked again to Raghav and asked.

Raghav answered by given the same expressionless look that scared Vivek. "I kill people." His way of speaking was slow and his voice was a little heavy and surly.

After hearing his answers Vivek was out of his senses. His eyes got widened. He turned to Raghav. Raghav also saw him. In ordinary cases, the answer is taken as a joke but Raghav's stance and appearance seemed dreadful. Moments after Raghav had a slight smile, that restored Vivek's senses.

Seeing him smiling, Vivek blew out his stuck breath from his mouth and said laughing. "Nice Joke. But you almost killed me."

Raghav looked straight onto the road and contrary to Vivek's expectation, he asked. "What about you?"

"I'm a photographer by profession. But..." He stretched 'but' till Raghav seemed to be intrigued. "I read people's mind by touching them, as a part time." Raghav seemed confused by Vivek's answer. Vivek looked at him and he smiled back, then took his eyes outdoors. "So now you're in the mood to joke." Raghav said.

"No! I am telling the truth."

"Well then," after responding, Raghav remain silent for a moment and then said again. "Touch my hand and tell what is going on in my mind." Raghav had his hand in front of Vivek.

Vivek looked at him and said hesitantly. "Right now?"

Raghav replied. "Yes, of course." He shook his hand in front of him. "Tell me what I'm thinking right now."

"O...Okay", Vivek agreed but did not seem confident.

Vivek touched Raghav's hands. After touching for a while, he pulled back his hand. He then, without uttering a single word, kept driving, focused on the road. Raghav did not understand this behaviour of Vivek's. He was expecting an answer from him. But Vivek was quiet and driving.

"What happened? You did not say anything." Asked Raghav.

Vivek saw Raghav and began to laugh. He answered Raghav laughing. "You are amazing. Do you think it's possible to read anyone's mind." Vivek kept laughing. "You cracked a joke. So did I."

"Huh.." Raghav responded fretfully.

Now they both were silent. Raghav was not already in the mood to talk and Vivek's mood was spoiled by Raghav.

After crossing Balco, Vivek's vehicle entered a city

named Korba. A small and beautiful town situated on Maikal ranges of Satpura Hills and Chota Nagpur Plateau is an open expanse. Hasdeo and Ahiran rivers flow through the city.

After advancing a little Raghav asked him to stop at a corner. Vivek stopped the car. Raghav grabbed his bag and got off the car. He went ahead without turning.

"Freaky Man! Not even a Thank You." Vivek said fretfully. There was a local theatre named Niharika in front. Raghav walked for a while and enter a narrow alley.

After watching him for sometime Vivek immediately took out a small notebook from the storage compartment and pulled a pen from his front pocket. He opened the notebook. It was a blank notebook. He rolled over some starting pages of the notebook in which some sketches were made. After flipping eight-ten pages he stopped at a blank page. He opened the lid of the pen and began to make something on the right page of the notebook.

Vivek's lips started stuttering. He was speaking in a low voice and at the same time was making something on the page. The nib of the pen was making a picture of a man. Vivek drew him a shirt, jacket and jeans wear and then started to make the second man on the next page. He gave the second man coat-wearing pajamas. He also made fine lines on his face. Perhaps it was the picture of an elderly man.

The pace was too fast to make sense of these images. He speaks the words as quickly as soon as the picture was complete. It took him only twenty seconds to make so far. He made a shotgun in the hands of the man in the jacket. He then stopped the drawing. The drawing was completed.

He looked carefully at the picture. His eyes widened with surprise and fear. "Hell no." He said.

He had made the two men on those two pages. The jacket wearing man was pointing a gun at the other man the images were blurred somewhere but clear enough to understand. It was like layouts but with details somewhere, especially faces were clear, hairstyle scars, wrinkles, beard and all important things were clearly visible.

Vivek had observed the direction of Raghav. He parked his vehicle in front of the theatre, locked it and entered into the colony where he saw Raghav. After few steps, there was a road turning right. Raghav was leading on that way. Vivek started following him silently. Meanwhile, he pulled his cell phone out from his pocket and dialed a number.

"Hello...Nikhil." He said.

"Yes Vivek. What happened?" It was the voice of Nikhil from the other side.

"Come to Niharika immediately! A murder is about to happen."

Chapter two

Slipped away

* * *

Time: morning 09:00 am.

Nikhil had some work in the police station. Unlike other officers he was in civil dress. He was dis-cussing with an officer before him. Amit Nayak, he was an inspector, looking for something in a register.

"Nayak!" Said Nikhil. Amit raised his head in an immediate reaction to the call of Nikhil.

"Yes sir." Nikhil gestured Amit to come along with him. "But sir, what about this case?" Amit said, pointing to the paper that he had put on the table. "It is more important than that case. Verma will handle that case." Said Nikhil.

On the main gate of the police station, the board said 'Rampur Police Station.' They both came out of there.

An SUV was parked at the police station. Amit sat in the driving seat and Nikhil sat next to him. "Ni-harika. Quick." Nayak started the vehicle and drove as fast as he could.

At the beginning, Nikhil was stunned to hear such a news from the mouth of Vivek. But he believed in Vivek. He immediately moved for Naharika as per Vivek's message.

Nikhil and Vivek were in contact with each oth-er through the mobile. Vivek had eyes on Raghav. He told

Nikhil about the meeting with Raghav in brief and at the same time maintained a sufficient distance while watching Raghav's activity.

Within five minutes they reached Niharika talkies. Vivek asked Nikhil to switch off the siren which could alert Raghav. Vivek appeared to them. Amit stopped the vehicle and approached him.

"Where is he?" Nikhil asked Vivek.

Vivek responded by indicating to the top of the first floor of a house which was at a short distance from him. "There! I just saw him entering there, after interrogating an old man." Vivek said and the three progressed.

There were plenty of shops where people were busy shopping and were engaged in daily routine. Presence of few health clinics also caused the crowd. The bikes were lined outside the clinic due to the which only road was left for pedestrians which was also choked-full because of pedestrians themself.

The three were still on one side of the road. According to Vivek, Raghav had entered an apartment adjacent to the road on the other side. They come near the house as mentioned by Vivek. It was the house right next to a tea stall. It had an opened shutter that went up the stairs.

They slowly started to increase their steps on the stairs. Nikhil was on forefront, Amit behind him and Vivek was on last. He prepared himself for any uncertain incident that could happen. Nikhil and Amit had their guns out. Their fingers were set on the trigger. The three were moving forward adjacent to the wall. On climbing a little, some old songs were heard. This confused them. Stairs ended up to a door on the right. The door was open, due to which the sound of the song was more audible. The volume of the song stifled the sound of the footsteps. First Nikhil entered in and Amit followed him. Vivek was held out.

"Oh no!" Nikhil's voice came from inside. Vivek also entered on his voice. He went inside and saw that a man in his forties was resting on Nikhil's lap. The blood was oozing out from his chest turned his shirt creating red spots. There were deep injuries on the forehead. Television was in the front in which song was playing on full volume. Amit switched off television first. Vivek quickly went to the man and held him.

The pain on his face could be seen clearly. He was groaning and trying to say something. Nikhil and Vivek were trying to understand him but he could not say anything correctly.

Before they could figure out something the man had died. "No!" Nikhil said.

Amit quickly examined the entire room. He found no one in the entire house. His steps stopped at the open window of that room.

"On the way, I heard about a man with long hair wearing a black jacket from sir." He said.

Listening to his voice Vivek Immediately came to him. Amit fingered out from window showing the signs of a man. "Is that him?"

"Yes he is." Vivek replied. "But he has gone too far."

The window that opens directly on the other side of the main street was. Raghav's back profile was es-tab-lished in the mind of Vivek. He had escaped out of the window and was walking among the crowd.

After Vivek said "yes", Amit looked down to the

window and gestured Vivek to step a side and said "I don't think so." Vivek didn't understand this act of Amit. Amit took his step back quickly and before Nikhil and Vivek could sense he ran, folded his knees and had jumped out from window. The window was big and wide. Before jumping, Amit had taken approx-imate measurements of window.

His body went down, landed properly on the ground. Amit got up and ran.

"This is so amazing." Vivek uttered while watch-ing the whole act of Amit. He immediately looked here and there and then he took out his belt from jeans.

"What are you doing?" Asked Nikhil.

In front, there was a thick and strong wire con-nected to the poles. He framed his belt in the wire and replied to Nikhil. "You see, I can't jump like him." Slid-ing through the wire with help of the belt he reached down, his burden sagged the wire.

Vivek got up, dusted off his jacket and ran be-hind Raghav. Activities of both caught attention of peo-ple around. But the best part was that Raghav was not interested in street affairs and walked straight. Amit had reached far enough. Running sound could alert Raghav so after running some distance Amit stopped running. He was moving quickly to follow him.

Vivek saw these smart move of Amit. After run-ning at some distance he started to walk quickly too. Maintaining his speed, Vivek was reaching near Raghav. Amit took out his gun from his waist. He was aiming at the Raghav's knee and pointed his gun to-wards that. Unfortunately, just then some people passed in between them and he was covered by them. Amit took out his finger from the trigger.

He again aimed at Raghav, but just then Raghav turned back, he saw Amit aiming his gun at him. Without losing any second, he immediately ran among the crowd. Amit ran after him. Raghav pulled his gun out of right side of his waist and fired two bullets down the street.

The sound of gunfire caused a rampage. Everyone was pounding wildly. Vehicles sped up. Amit and Vivek rushed behind Raghav but the crowd offered resistance. When the crowd dispersed, they found that Raghav had escaped. Both of them lost Raghav. Amit and Nikhil left staring each other's face. They were left with no other choice than moving back to that house.

Chapter three
Investigation begins

* * *

Time : morning 10.00 am.

After Raghav slipped out, Amit and Vivek came back. The neighbours had already started whispering in each other's ears. Everyone, looking at the police's action, failed in his attempt to understand. Their voices seemed like the buzzing of a mosquito. Women, despite scared, were engaged in their entertainment. They had a new topic to discuss apart from backbiting each other. A sub-inspector was telling the crowd to stay at arm's length. The ambulance had reached. They were starting their job. Below here, Inspector Amit Nayak stood near the shutter door where a few people were interrogated.

The view of the room was full of hustle and bustle. A man was making a map around the dead body with a white chalk. Stretcher for carrying the corpse was being brought up.

Nikhil was trying to understand the whole scene where the incident took place while Vivek was standing behind him was thinking some-thing. He didn't know the dead man but his face expression said that he was felt kind of a guilty for not saving him. Nikhil understood his feelings but he was unable to do anything at that moment.

Nikhil got back to work. He took his glasses out of his eyes with handkerchiefs to clean the glasses, fogged it up with his breath, wiped again and wore them back.

"First, he would have knocked the door." Nikhil started suggesting possibilities. He turned towards the door. All the attention was on his side. "As soon as the door opened, Raghav attacked him with his shotgun on his head." Nikhil pointed out to the injury on dead man's head and blood coming out from there. He was telling this all so confidently like it's visuals were moving in front of him.

Nikhil came to the table and looked down at the table's leg. There had some scratches on the floor. It was easy to guess that the table in its place had a sudden displacement. "He staggered from that attack and stumbled to the table." All officers were listening to him attentively.

"Raghav picked him from here and hit him on the wall." Nikhil went along a three-seater sofa, which was in front of a table, to the wall which had blood stains. "Then he might have increased the volume of the television and before he could recoup, he tossed him again there." Nikhil said seeing blood stains on the floor.

After saying that, he came to the showcase placed below the television. "He probably came here after injuring him. The books are messed up here other stuff are also demolished. Looks like he was searching for something."

So saying, he asked an officer, shouting. "Salim! Did you find something in the bedroom or kitchen?"

"No, sir!" Came the answer from the bedroom in a thunderous voice.

Nikhil heard the answer and pulled out a packet of cashew from the right pocket of his shirt. Tore it and began to eat. "He killed him by his gun, it means... he might have used a silencer in his gun that's why no sound of firing was heard." He said as he ate. Chewing of cashew was matching the rhythm of his words.

"Sir!! look at this." An officer came and said to Nikhil. A white wig, fake beard and fake mustache were in his hand. Nikhil's eye was on that. Officer read the question of his face and answered. "These are the dead body's fake hair, beard and mustache."

Seeing this, bells started ringing in the minds of Nikhil and Vivek. They went near the corpse. Two fingers were zipping the dead body up, Nikhil's hand stopped them when they were about to cover up the face completely. Looking the corpse's face carefully Nikhil started to think of something.

"Perhaps I have seen him before." Vivek said fixing his jacket.

"If I'm not mistaken, He is...Dr. Sumit Bhardwaj a scientist in the world of chemical sciences." Said Nikhil. Cashews were affecting his memory powers for sure.

"Yes!! It is him...But why were they staying here in disguise?" Vivek questioned and without waiting for an answer from anyone he said himself. “No!!”

“What happened?” Asked Nikhil. Vivek immediately took out his cell phone from his pocket and opened the Internet. Shortly after opening few pages on the browser tabs he said to Nikhil, pointing to the screen. “Look at this.”

Nikhil looked carefully at the screen. It was a news published on 30th April 2014. “He was one of the scientists of Shivraam Labs.” Vivek said. He looked at the five men standing on the screen. One of the people in the photograph matched exactly with the deceased.

Vivek operated his mobile again and showed him the page on the second tab and said. “He is Rama Tan-don, a member of the team. Around five-six months ago he was murdered too. The murderer hasn't been found yet.” He paused and said. “Do you know what does that mean?”

Nikhil said while turning towards him. “You want to say the rest of them would also be killed.”

Vivek replied. “You can guess, as the situation suggests so.” They could sense that there was something very serious and big.

Nikhil shouted. “Salim!” A sub-inspector immediately attended to him. “Sir!” He came to Nikhil and stood at attention.

It was weird but Vivek was kind of enjoying that calling name and standing in attention thing. It never happens to all that his friend commanding to others where they obey him.

Nikhil ordered Salim. “I want all the information about these scientists and Shivraam labs. Where did they live? What did they do? The family and everything that appears to be suspicious. I want their details in half an hour." This order from Nikhil and his tone to his junior confirmed Vivek that not only Nikhil understood the seriousness of the situation but was also not going to take it lightly.

"Yes Sir!" Sub-inspector responded quickly and went by. Salim's instant action on that signaled Vivek that his juniors also knew Nikhil's imprescriptible about the case.

"Let's go down. Maybe Amit..." Nikhil stopped his words, Vivek was sketching something on opened pages of a copy in front of him. Nikhil's eyes turned left right while he looked at his team. No one was watching Vivek. Nikhil got relaxed. He went to him. Vivek was drawing something like he had drawn previously.

Vivek had completed the picture. He turned to Nikhil showing front page, said. "When I held the doctor I saw these things which were going on in his mind."

"Sardar and Tables? Well, but what does this mean?" By looking at the page said Nikhil. Vivek had sketched the face of a Sardar and a table arrangement was made on the next page. Nikhil took that copy from his hand. Looking at these pictures, he was puzzled. "... And this is the logo of Sivaram Labs. Isn't it?" looking at the sign at the bottom of the page, said Nikhil.

"Now what?" Vivek asked.

Nikhil pushed back his glasses to his nose, blew out a sigh and said in a poetic style. "Sardard namuraad mehbooba si ho chali hai, peechha chhod jaane ka ahsaas karakar dobara laut aati hai. Let's go down to know what Amit has found."

"Have tea.." Amit put down a cup full of tea on the table in front of a boy.

"Sir, aren't you gonna hit me after letting me have tea?" The boy picked up the cup and said hesitatingly.

"Do I look like goon cops?" Amit said in his thunder voice. Apparently, he was a harsh policeman, owner of the flat and emotionless face. If the boy had the courage he surely would have said 'yes' but drank half the tea by in one go producing a 'surrr' sound instead.

"No offense sir, but that how it's depicted in the movies." The boy said.

Amit sat at the table with his tea and told him. "It seems you haven't watched a movie showing good policemen." Amit took the first sip of tea and asked him. "Do you know Sooraj, Why am I offering you tea?" Sooraj responded 'no' by shaking his head.

Amit took another sip and told him. "I interrogated everyone here but none of them know a single thing about 'the man'. Someone here told me that you roam around here all day. So I thought you would not let me down."

It was hard to tell by looking at the Amit's style of interrogation whether he was being nice or trying to torture but it indicated certainly that he had his own way to digging out information.

Sooraj's face became pale, he placed the teacup on the table and said. "Well, sir! I know nothing about that man. He was a ghost. He always remained inside the house like it was his only world. Yes! I sometimes saw him going to the restaurant near Ghantaghar and that too alone." Sooraj spoke out all in one breath. And Amit succeeded to flush out information, little but better than nothing.

"Which restaurant?" Amit continued the interrogation.

Nikhil and Vivek came down at the same time. Amit instructed Sooraj to go. Nikhil went to Amit and asked. "Did you find something?"

"Nothing sir. People never saw him getting out of here and he appeared to be a cool kind of man. He didn't give any chance to the landlord to complain."

"Meeting somebody or going anywhere?"

"No. He hardly came out of the house. But he used to go to the 'punjabi restaurant', that boy had seen him there sometimes."

After hearing about the Punja-bi restaurant Nikhil and Vivek's eyes stared each other. Nikhil understood what could be the next move at the moment. Amit was perplexed to understand their next move. Nikhil took that copy from Vivek's hand and tore that page in which Vivek had drawn a picture. He folded that page and kept it in his back pocket then said to Amit. "Let's move to that restaurant."

Amit got more confused by the 'page tearing' act. He looked at Vivek and asked Nikhil. "What is it, sir?" He was pointing at the page.

"Later..." Nikhil answered Amit avoiding the topic. He asked Amit and Vivek to follow him. The three began to take step towards their vehicles.

Two teams of news channels had arrived there for news. They were reporting till they saw Nikhil. The wait ended for they were thirsty for water. Reporters with their cameraman stood in front of Nikhil. It seemed like they were pouncing him. He responded with a satisfactory answer and assured them to solve the case soon.

Amit, walking behind Nikhil and Vivek, he stared at Vivek. He pulled out his cell phone without coming to the notice of both and wrote a message.

'We have a problem here.' After finished typing, he pressed the send button.

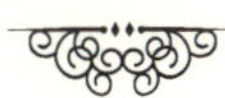

Chapter four

The first fish

* * *

Time : morning 10.30 am.

"Sumit Bhardwaj, Chandraprakash Rao, Rama Tandon, Akram Tripathi, David D'Souza." Vivek read the names of the five main members of Shivraam labs. All of them were chosen from different directions of India." He was holding his cell phone and the searched pages by google were on. It showed an old news, These people in the year 2014 in UP, in some backward village, found a stone that was believed to be unique and useful. The team of scientists was about to begin a research on that stone. One and a half years later, one of their members Rama Tandon was shot dead. His body was found at his home. Today, six months later, another member was killed. Now the case was taken up by Nikhil in his account.

After Vivek told the details of the news to Nikhil and Amit, the three sat on their respective vehicles.

Vivek was coming behind Nikhil and Amit. According to Sooraj, the boy who was interrogated by Amit, that Punjabi restaurant was a short walk away.

Amit was driving and Nikhil was on the phone, instructing in a hard voice. "Listen carefully Deepak! Salim is searching their history. After the details are known it is your job to inform their family of their death. Understood? ....Good! bye!"

Google did no help much apart from telling their names. After filtering google they didn't find any useful information about that stone and its experiments. Only got the news of the death of just one member. The idea of others being in danger did not seem too wrong.

Amit stopped his vehicle outside the Ghanta Ghar complex. "Reached." Amit said to Nikhil. Vivek stopped his Scorpio behind them. They got off their respective vehicles and parked their vehicle a short distance from the restaurant.

Ghantaghar was one of the most beautiful and well-known places in Korba town. The best thing was that complex was in circular shape. Shops were there on both sides. For entering inside there were three opening. Opposite to inner, on outer faced area almost all shops were hired. But the actual reason for the place being famous was a big and a long structure inside the center. In the top of the structure, there were four big-square-shaped clocks for each direction mounted on a cylindrical pillar supported by a thin pillar. Some more geometrical structures were below, supporting this structure was dignifying the crossroad. The structure itself was surrounded by a circular shape drain in which water was falling down and also occupied by small park like arrangement which was making it more beautiful.

This internal design, leaving little space, was itself covered with another circular sitting arrangement, another gem on Ghantaghar for praising its beauty. It was morning time, therefore, there were no one sitting here.

The restaurant was on the road, on the front facing direction of the complex. The main door was made of glass and had four steps at the entry. Entering from the door, on the right was the main cash counter where a Sardar was sitting. In front of it was a line of table and chairs had been arranged. There were few round tables surrounded by four chairs and some long tables at the corners that could accommodate more people.

Nikhil looked at the face of the Sardar and pulled that page from his back pocket. He looked at the sketch and then looked up at his face again. Even thought Nikhil knew about the powers of Vivek, he was little surprised. But on the other hand, Amit was astonished because Vivek had made a face that was almost matching with Sardar's and this was still a big question for Amit messing around with his head.

After entering there, the Sardar's hand politely gestured and asked them to sit on the chairs. Ignoring his request Amit reached him. This time at the restaurant, only two-three people had come to eat. They were busy among themselves as the three appeared to be usual customers.

Amit pulled out his mobile from his pocket and showed him a picture. "Do you recognize him?" asked Amit.

Sardar took mobile from Amit's hand and brought it nearer to his eyes. "Yes, of course. He had come here three or four times. But..." He squeezed his eyebrows and looked at the picture and said. "Why did he pose for the photograph with closed eyes?" Sardar asked naively. It was the picture of doctor's dead body.

Amit put his mobile back in his pocket and keeping a serious tone, replied. "He got murdered a while ago."

On listening, a wave of fear went through his

body. He stood still with his jaw open. “Now you will tell the truth. How do you know him?” Said Nikhil instilling fear into the already frightened Sardar. He was the last thing in Dr. Sumit’s head made him a suspect.

“I... I am absolutely telling the truth sir ji.” Sardar was a little scared. Nikhil eyes signaled Vivek. Vivek understood Nikhil’s gesture. He went to the Sardar and put a hand on his shoulder. It was the idea of reading Sardar’s mind.

“Tell the truth Paaji otherwise if their mind gets messed up, they’ll mess you up.” Vivek tried to scare the Sardar a little more.

He was a lanky young boy, unlike other Sardars. The presence of the three was enough to scare him, as every normal person would be who had never faced any matter with police. But his answer didn’t change. “He always came alone, used to seat there and after eating his favorite ‘Paalak-Paneer used to go quietly.” He was completing his word.

Vivek removed his hand from his shoulder and slightly moved his head in ‘no’ as he looked at Nikhil. Amit saw the gestures but was forced to ignore the fact.

Nikhil went to Vivek and whispered. “Why did the scientist think about this Sardar in his last breath?”

Vivek also responded whispering. “I’m wondering what is the connection of these two? Or may be..”

“Or maybe what?”

“Maybe he thought just about the restaurant. Sardar’s image would have crept along with the restaurant.” Vivek had reasonable point.

The seating arrangement was similar to the rest of the restaurant. Such as local train. Two chairs on either side of a table. The first chair and second chair were positioned adjacent to each other. Third and fourth chair positioned in front of the second and first chair respectively. Sardar's finger was pointing to the chair number four of the second table.

Vivek had gone the same way. He looked at the table and asked the Sardar. "Are you sure?"

"Hundred percent sir ji." Sardar replied confidently.

Vivek's eye was looking down at the third table. He raised his eyes and looked at Nikhil and Amit one by one. He said. " The second member is here."

Listening to Vivek, Amit and Nikhil's eyes widened. "How can you say?" Asked Nikhil immediately.

"Come here and see for yourself." He called them in front of the first chair of the third table and put his hand on the table. "Look at this." According to chair's arrangement, this chair was behind doctor Sumit's chair.

Amit and Nikhil understood everything after seeing that. 'S' the sign of Shivraam labs was scratched with a key on table same as Vivek had drawn on the page. "If he was sitting there, then who made the 'logo' here?"

Now the two understood what exactly was go-ing on in Sumit's head when he was dying.

"At what time they used to come?" asked Nikhil to raise his voice a little. "Around this time." Sardar replied after thinking.

"Maybe he had been come here to meet his members." Vivek supposed.

"Maybe." said Nikhil after thinking a while. "We have to find out. "

Nikhil came back to Sardar after whispering

something in Amit and Vivek's ears and explained him something too.

Nikhil was talking with Sardar and Vivek sat on the fourth chair of the third table. Just in front of the chair where the next member was expected to come. Amit sat in the second chair of the first table, he was served with Dosa. Nikhil took a cold drink and sat on fourth number chair of first table, diagonal to Amit.

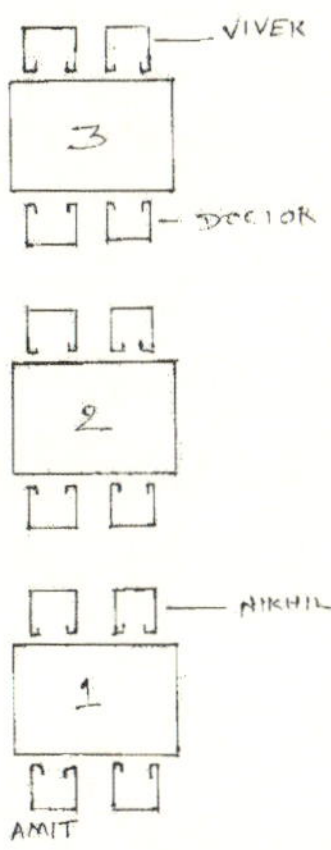

Now they were waiting for the arrival of the next member. Nobody came within ten minutes. The eyes of the three were still at the door. Vivek took out his mobile and started reading that news carefully suddenly a middle-aged man sat on the chair in front of him.

He was looking at the man carefully. The man, in every few minutes, kept on checking the time on his watch, so it was clear that he was waiting for someone. He could see the discomfort on his face. Vivek had well remembered the rest of the scientists face of the Shivraam labs. Seeing his face he was trying to understand his true identity. He reopened the tab on his mobile for the convenience and then began matching the face. The pair of eyes had a thick black frame, that he pushed to the forehead at intervals with his fingers. Less hair on the head and dark complexion. Light blue shirt and black pants, he was wearing.

"Dr. Chandraprakash. Of course, he is Dr. Chandraprakash." Thought Vivek after closely inspecting the facial features of the man. He was fully assured.

****

6 months ago from today. July 2015.

"Now what will we do, sir?" Dr. Akram said. He seemed quite nervous and scared. "What if whatever the old man, who we met at the village while searching for this stone, told is true."

"No need to fear Akram! And speak more quietly!" Dr. Sumit tried to calm him. He was sitting in the chair next to him. Dr. David on right side of Dr. Sumit and Chandraprakash were sitting left to Dr. Akram. Wrinkle ridges appeared on their faces.

"In the lab, we have none other than us. Let him talk". Seventy-five-year-old's voice was hard. He was Shivraam Dharmatma, founder of Shivraam Labs. His hairs were gray, but the ageing of the body did not become a stumbling block in the strength and wellness. Despite covered with clothes and a coat, his body shape was looking well maintained. His face was reflecting a very strong attraction. He sat on the other side of the table in front of those four. "I can understand your fear.

A week ago, Dr. Rama was murdered and I know why."

On hearing this, every face started questioning. Shivraam added. "Whoever the killer was, he had come to take the stone, it is for the test results and all the data. I handed all that to Dr. Rama on his murder night but the killer didn't get anything."

"How can you say that, sir?" David asked. "Because just before going back he returned all that to me. He did not consider himself worthy of this responsibility."

David said. "It means there is somebody else who knows what can that stone do."

"Yes! Maybe somebody from the lab. I have to find him. Till then it is more important to save you people." Shivraam said. "Now you all listen carefully what I am about to tell." He took out four packets from a table drawer. Sticker was affixed over these packets of each scientist. He laid packets of their respective names in front of them.

"This...What is this, sir?" Dr. Sumit asked. Shivraam walked towards the window and peeping at the greenery outside he said "An attempt to save the life of all of you. You know how serious the matter is. Not simply because your lives are at stake, but something else is at stake which is more important than you people's lives. So you all have to leave your homes...today." When they heard this, they started to look each other.

Shivraam turned to them and said. "Only one person couldn't keep all experiment data, so I divide it into four part and put it in the pen drive. The packets contain your new address and a new name, with a new appearance. No one is allowed to know others name and address. You all have to do this otherwise you all will die. It also has mobile. Use it only if there is any emergency."

"But, sir! After all, this what if our enemy know about us?" Worried Dr. Akram asked.

"I have even thought for that. You all will meet secretly once in a week for well being of each other without telling each other's address and name. I know you are expert in this. If something happens to anyone, the remaining immediately change their place. Nothing to worry about. I'll keep an eye on each of you. Nothing's going to happen to you till I am alive."

"But sir! What about our family?" David said.

They all had families except Dr. Chandraprakash. Shivraam assured them all and said. "Do not worry. The news will reach them tomorrow."

"And where is that stone?" Dr. David asked. "It will be safe with me." Shivraam assured all.

Everyone seemed to agree. They all grabbed their respective packets and went out from there.

Chapter five

The race begins

* * *

Time : morning 11.00 am today.

Vivek had concealed his face under the menu card. The moment the man looked at Vivek, Vivek continued looking in the menu. Vivek had gestured Amit. However, after telling Nikhil, Amit was waiting for his instructions to take that man into custody. Am-it's eyes sought permission to Nikhil for this by meeting his eyes, but Nikhil shook his head and refused.

There was an L.C.D. on the wall in right side of Vivek's table. A local news channel was on. Dr. Sum-it's killing footage was just showing on that news. The man saw and immediately stood from his place. He looked scared and upset. He turned to go back. Amit held his pistol strongly and was about to stand but Nikhil, moving finger, gestured him to sit again. Amit was wearing a uniform, therefore, the man crossed the door by giving him a look.

"Had he doubted Amit?" Asked Vivek after approaching Nikhil. It was justified to doubt. Nikhil was watching him sitting in a car on the road. As he sat in his car the three quickly exited from the restaurant.

"No! He doesn't know that we know. He just ran because of the news of his friend's death." Nikhil replied.

"We have to go in your car Vivek! If he sees a police vehicle behind him, he will get suspicious of us." Said Nikhil and both began to move towards Vivek's Scorpio.

"Sir! Why did not you let me catch him?" Amit asked, climbing down, out of confusion about the Nikhil's movement in the restaurant.

Nikhil replied, reaching out to the car. "To reach the end, have to grab the chain and climb up, not break!" Nikhil tried came out with a metaphor. He added further. "Now he will guide us to other members. If our theory is correct, then we must locate them all before Raghav."

Nikhil opened the door and sat in the driving seat. Vivek also entered by the other side and sat next to him. Amit sat on the back seat.

Nikhil had seen car number carefully so they were following him. They had maintained enough distance.

Then the Salim called Nikhil. Salim was quick in his job and his network was also very strong. Nikhil picked up the call of Salim and listened to the breakthroughs for a while from the other side. Amit and Vivek were watching him curiously.

"Well! Do some more digging about them and report to me." Nikhil said to Salim before disconnecting the call. Nikhil Keeping his phone, Vivek said. "Got anything?"

Nikhil had mixed expressions of disappointment and amazement. "Nothing...and a lot."

After hearing such an answer, Vivek had the same expressions of amazement. Nikhil answered himself before anyone asked. "All of them started to disappear from their home after Rama Tandon's death. They just left a note."

"Note? What did it say?"

"That they all went to an unknown place for the safety of their family and they'll come back once everything gets all right."

This intrigued them even more and stirred them to know what's behind all this that was even more important. Suddenly the peace was disrupted when Amit cast a question. "Now I think you should tell me the truth."

"What truth?" Without turning his face Nikhil responded. "That how does your friend know that a murder is going to happen and what about that sketch?" In Amit's mind, these questions were bothering him. Yet he was unaware of Vivek. Hearing Amit's question.

Nikhil looked at him then he looked at Vivek. Vivek gave his assent. Nikhil had brought Amit with trust. Now was the time to rely on that trust.

Nikhil told Amit in detail about the Vivek's special feature. Amit's face was worth watching. The design of his face was exactly as when Nikhil learned this truth. He still was not able to be sure of that. With his left hand rested on his knee, palm supporting his chin, he was staring at the Vivek. Vivek looked at him through the rearview mirror and he smiled.

Seeing Amit like this, It reminded Vivek even his expression when he first came to know about his extraordinary skills, When he was at the age of 12.

"Call your parents tomorrow. We'll talk to them."

Vivek was entering into the home when he heard this voice. It was his father's. Vivek just came from the ground after playing cricket. Holding the bat in right hand that laid on the shoulder, just like any another child who owns the bat. He had a blue colored cricket jersey on top, indicating his passion for cricket. Ease on his face mixed with happiness was signaling his victory of the match.

Walking inside the drawing room he saw a boy almost of the age of 25, sitting in front of his parents. Well dressed and well-behaving person as per his appearance. He was smiling and shaking his head as 'yes'. His 'bua', father's sister was standing behind her bedroom's door smiling and watching everything at the same time trying to hide.

Vivek understood that the boy was his bua's special friend who was the trending topic on his home nowadays. They all were seemed happy. This was the sign of things gone well between them. That boy stood from the chair and joined his hand in a respective manner, did a 'Namaste'. Coming toward the door he saw Vivek.

"That's Vivek. our son." Vivek's father Devesh introduced him.

"Wow! Future's next Sachin Tendulkar." That

boy bowed a little bit and said, messing his hairs. He said further putting a hand on his shoulder. "I also wanted to became a famous cricketer, but you know how life has it's own plans for you."

"Ya." Devesh responded smiling. He came near to him and departed him.

"What is happening to you bittu?" Devesh was waving his hand, saying goodbye to the boy when his wife's voice distracted him. That boy had left by then.

Devesh instantly turned to that direction. He saw his son sweating and hands shivering. He could see the little drops of sweats on his forehead and the upper lip above. He, at the drop of a hat, ran towards him and took out his kerchief to wipe. Vivek's bua had also reached near and wiped him.

"What happened son?" He asked Vivek anxiously.

Vivek tried to stop his hand and said. "That same thing I have been telling you about."

His mother and bua started looking to Devesh with questions on their faces.

Devesh stood staring at Vivek's hand. Devesh's finger was pointing to Vivek, said. "It is shivering in a pattern I think. Hang on a second."

Devesh quickly went to Vivek's bedroom. Some moment passed, he came out holding a copy and a pencil in his hand. There was a table in front of the three seater chair they have been sitting. Devesh put that copy on the table and handed pencil to Vivek on his oscillating right.

"Let out what your hands are trying to tell."

He said.

Vivek's mother, Anamika and bua Charulata were still swimming in the ocean of surprise. They were forced to do nothing but see.

The three were constantly gazing at him. It took fifteen minutes when Vivek seized his hand.

"It's impaired." Watching Vivek's complete picture, Devesh said. There were distorted lines on the page trying to make any particular shape but unsuccessful.

"Try again." Devesh flipped that page and opened a new one, moved aside to Vivek and said. Vivek tried one more time. This time it was visible that it's a picture of a boy and a girl hugging each other but still not recognizable.

"One more." Devesh again flipped that page and pass it to Vivek. He tried again. This time sketch was more clear.

"He is looking like Avee." Charulata identified the boy in the picture. She tried to recognize girl too but couldn't.

Devesh turned that page too and gestured Vivek. Vivek took the hint and started sketching. After hard work of one and a half hour and making three more pictures of distorted faces Vivek got upset.

Devesh put his hand on Vivek's back and said in an inspiring way. "Close your eyes son. Let free yourself, away from distractions and pressure. Don't listen to anything and focus on your visions. Let your thoughts think of the shapes and draw."

Vivek did the same as his father said. He closed his eyes, concentrated to visions. After two minutes he opened his eyes and finally made a clean and clear sketch.

Charulata's hand automatically covered his mouth. "That's Shikha, my friend." She said watching the girl hugging Avee.

That boy was Avee who came to their house to discuss his engagement with Charulata. Devesh accepted his proposal. But this picture was telling another story.

"I know this tree. It's from 'ujjwal park' where I hate to go." She said recognizing the tree behind them.

A clear expression of anger emerged on Devesh's face. "Let's go." He grabbed Charulata's hand and took her with him.

Vivek and his mother Anamika kept looking them. One hour later, they came back. Charulata had dry tears in her eyes. Anamika went to her and held her. She took her to her bedroom then came back.

"Vivek! You go to your room and do your homework." Devesh said. Vivek was surprised and curious but he also knew that this was not the best time to ask his father for details.

He silently went to his bedroom, closed the door and stuck his right ear on the door to listen to the talks. He heard some voices of his father and mother.

"Avee was cheating on Charu with her friend Shikha. We caught him red handed with her in Ujjwal park. Shikha also didn't know about his games. I rejected his proposal as a hard slap on his face. He'll never bother Charu and us again." That was Devesh's voice.

"Thank God! Bittu saved Charu's life from being be ruined. But how? How does he picture that?" Anamika's voice. "He is not even good in drawing. He got eight out of twenty-five in the subject. How can he make pictures that clear?" She added. She was now a question box locked by surprises.

"Do you remember that Vivek has this sweating and shivering issues since 7 and complaining about blurred images?"

"Yes! We consulted doctors also but they had no idea." Anamika answered.

"These images are not blurred anymore. As per Vivek, he sees some negatives image slightly clear when someone touches him or come in contact."

"What do you want to say, Vivek ke papa?" She mentioned him in a typical Indian wife style. "How... how is that possible? Our son...our son??..."

"...Is very special Anamika." Devesh interrupted in the middle and finished her sentence. "Our son has special gifts. Gift of sixth sense of high level with artistic quality. Not only he can read minds and sense future by seeing visuals but also can make sketches of that."

"What??" Vivek eyes got widened here.

"Sir, when and how did you know about these powers?" Lost in his childhood thoughts, this question of Amit took Vivek back to present moment. Amit had reached a blank world of thought. He brought his senses back and with an astonishing expression.

"Some other time." Said Nikhil and ignored.

Vivek suddenly exclaimed in the middle. "Recalling that memory. How's your girlfriend Payal?" Hearing Payal's name Nikhil started looking at Vivek like he remembered something. "What happened? Why are you looking like this?" Vivek asked.

"Payal! Payal!...Thanks for reminding." Nikhil extracted mobile from the pocket. "I had forgotten that every hour of every day I have to message a 'sorry'." He quickly typed in his mobile, put it back into the pocket and said facing Vivek. "You saved me today."

"Your mind should not wander far from the case because of Payal." Vivek quipped.

Vivek took care that his car was not visible to the doctor. They were still moving the same way. Suddenly Nikhil stopped the car. Vivek saw a man in front of the road stood with a black Scorpio. After descending from the vehicle, Nikhil asked Vivek to get back to driving seat and proceed. Vivek was puzzled but the sight of the car had not to be lost so he moved forward.

After single following the car for a while, Vivek saw to his right. That black Scorpio had come right next to him. This time Nikhil was in the driving seat and Amit sat beside him. Nikhil was already in civil dress. This time Amit had changed his clothes too. From the window his white shirt was visible. He had worn black goggles in the face. Nikhil arranged a vehicle for their own from his sources.

Surely, he had changed at the backside, and then came forward, therefore, Nikhil is driving now. Thought echoed in Vivek's mind. "In appearance, he looks like Raghav's brother. Just does not have a beard on his face and the hair is not that long. But face expressions and stature matches."

After almost one and a half hour of fast driving, they entered town named Bilaspur. Which is famous for having 3rd cleanest and 4th longest railway station in India, well known for its rich, varied and colorful culture. The local cuisine is well known for 'Samosas of nitti' and 'parotha of chikka'. But it was confirmed that they aren't going to get a chance to taste those.

Going forward, they arrived at Ganesh Chowk. "It's Nehru Nagar, we have reached." Amit said when they infiltrated a colony. After taking a right and two left turns that car stopped in front of a three-storey house. Vivek and Nikhil stopped their car on a turn outside of a house and took it back. The man came down from the car and went into the house.

Amit put his hand on the door handle to open the lock just then Nikhil had stopped holding his hand. "What happened, sir? Are we not going to catch him?" Amit said.

"No! Look at that." Nikhil pointed to the car in front of him. "There is the parking but he did not park it there that means he's going to go somewhere else." Amit understood Nikhil and applied a break on his ardency.

After some ten minutes of waiting, the man came back down. He was alone. He sat in the car and began to come towards their side. The three of them had already been prepared for it. Amit was next to the driving seat, so he turned his head, which made it hard to see his face. Nikhil had the simplest thing to do, he pretended to be asleep by putting the napkin on the face. Vivek acted to tie his shoelace out of the car. They waited for the car to go till they took a turn. As it turned, the three quickly took their place, like someone may have touched their live wire. Nikhil and Vivek turned their car and once again the chase has begun.

Time: 1:00 pm, Afternoon. Magneto Mall.

"I think he called the remaining members for a meeting? If I'm right." Said Nikhil.

On chasing the man, whom Vivek hoped to be Dr. Chandraprakash, they reached the mall. They parked their vehicles on the other side of the road. On seeing the man moving towards the mall they hurried to follow him inside the mall. Showing his ID card to the security guard. Nikhil entered with both of them.

Nikhil said. "Both of you, be together, I'll cover the lift path." And he went away from them. Seeing the direction of the doctor he has chosen a way of making it easy to monitor and work to be tackled.

The doctor took the escalator for going from ground floor to the first floor. Nikhil moved to the nearest lift that was all ready to go up. The doctor reached to the first floor when Nikhil and Vivek had just kept their foot on the escalator.

"Where has he gone?" When they reach the first floor startled Vivek uttered.

The doctor had gone invisible. The path was leading to the crowd. They immediately saw the right-left where the area was small, even the crowd was less there. So, Amit decided to go ahead. "let's move forward." Vivek agreed with Amit. Both progressed.

"Wait!!" After advancing a few steps, Vivek stopped Amit by grabbing his hand.

"What happened?" Amit said. Without answering, Vivek first looked behind and the next moment he turned his face to straight. Wrinkle ridges emerged on his face.

"Raghav is behind us." Vivek said.

Chapter six

Face to face

* * *

"What do we do now?" Vivek said in worried tones. They were still moving to find the man. Amit knew any misstep in a crowded place can put people in danger, so he asked Vivek to keep walking.

"We must take him out from the public." Amit replied.

"How?"

Amit did not respond, just kept walking forward. His gaze fell on some boys coming from the front and suddenly changed his thinking expression. He grabbed the hand of Vivek and said. "I will go after him, you just create a ruckus."

"What do you mean?..." Asked Vivek meanwhile a boy talking, on his cell phone, was approaching towards him. Before Vivek could say anything Amit let Vivek's hand on that boy's cheek. The slap was very hard and echoed there. Since the boys were busy in their own fun, therefore, they did not know that Amit was behind all this.

This act of Amit created a small uproar. Giving evidence of their solid friendship the two friends walking with the boy began to punt Vivek into a debate. Melee started.

Crowd's focus was on the fight. People, redeeming duty, began to gather because it was the chance for them to enjoy a show without a ticket for free and they didn't want to let it go. After all, people don't get a chance to see a live fight every day.

Raghav, like always had no interest in it. He looked back just for a moment. Fortunately, Vivek was covered between the crowd so he did not appear to Raghav. Raghav went next through Amit. Passing Raghav, Amit got behind him.

How he brought a shotgun in? The question pops out on Amit's mind when a gun started to peep out of from Raghav's jacket, which was resting comfortably on his belt.

Letting Vivek in trouble, Amit had successfully executed his plan as one side of the crowd was busy enjoying the show. Raghav was now going to the next crowd. It was time for Amit. He quickly came behind Raghav and raised his hand to hit him. Amit, at this point, realized Raghav's circumspective when Raghav stopped him immediately and punched him back very strongly in return. Amit has bagged two steps back.

Amit handled himself and looked at Raghav. Raghav stood before him. Both of their eyes trapped inside the goggles were judging each other. Amit tilted his neck to right. The sound of Amit's snapping vein of neck hinted his readiness for the fight. Both moved fast towards each other. Amit tilting down, saved himself from Raghav's punch and punched on his stomach. Raghav has retreated a few steps. This was his answer to be wise. Before Raghav could recover Amit gave somersault in the air and made and egregious hit on his face.

Amit moved forward to hit Raghav. He attacked at him with his foot. Raghav prevented his attack by the leg. Amit same time tried to hit him with his right hand, but Raghav, with his left hand, also immediately stopped the attack. Amit, before he could do another attack, Raghav hit a strong punch in the face of Amit. Amit's entire body was shaking. He stood recouping himself when Raghav's next kick delivered him in the rear gift store, gave it's owner the money trauma, breaking its glass. Amit's goggles hit the floor out of his face.

Vivek also came to fight him. Raghav, to avoid Vivek's punch again bent himself and thrown him to Amit when he was standing. Vivek collided with Amit and they were slammed on the floor. Both were lying on the floor together. They were just standing up and Raghav began to flee.

"Are you fine?" Vivek asked Amit took hold. Co-incidently, Their similar looking handsets fell. They both picked up their mobiles.

Both were comfortable now but Amit was more hurt. He did take some more time to recover, which Vivek could not give to Raghav. He saw Raghav running on escalator began to escalate quickly. The escalator was quite at a distance, Vivek saw a lift in front of him, a boy and a girl were in there. Which was all ready to go upward, it's door was closing. He ran towards there.

This small battle had alerted all. Both of them did not know that of these guys who is good and who is bad? The elevator was getting off and they did not need to stop it, for Vivek.

Running toward elevator Vivek, understood by

seeing fear and dreadful expressions of their faces that they aren't going to stop it for him. Lift door was closing. Now in less time and space, Vivek had to enter in lift between its doors that was very narrow. By running, Vivek did the math. He took a strong jump and bent his body at an angle chest part was rolled to his right shoulder forward. Now the space between the door and his body was of same of the width. Both his back and chest in a side door of the elevator entered rubbing. His right shoulder slammed against the glass wall of the other end of the elevator and he fell down.

He stood caressing his shoulder.

The boy and girl were watching him. This act of Vivek's slightly increased fear in them. Meanwhile, Amit composed himself and watched Raghav escaping. He had reached the second floor and was going to the escalator which takes him up to the third floor.

The elevator stopped on the second floor. Vivek quickly pressed the door off buttons of lift. The boy and the girl did not get a chance to get out. They got more afraid. At this point, Vivek was like a man with horns on the head for them. God knows when he's gonna turn and attack.

The door opened at the third floor Vivek quickly ran out with thunder speed. The girl and boy who were relieved immediately pressed the button to go down. Fortunately, Raghav was within the reach of Vivek.

Vivek took full advantage of this opportunity and ran. Raghav also saw Vivek and his running like a wounded lion-mode. He immediately took his shotgun. Before he would do anything, Vivek jumped on him. The shotgun fell from his hand.

Vivek had his knees over Raghav and began to rain punches on his face. Raghav prevented his attack after his four punches, reversed Vivek. Now Raghav thrust his knees over Vivek. He was in a hurry. His eyes fell on the Amit who was approaching the second floor. Raghav moved from the top and quickly raised his shotgun that had been lying nearby and pointed it at Vivek. Vivek stood slowly.

"I thought I would have to spend four bullets today. But I have to spend one more for free because of you." Raghav said.

The two stood next to the railing at the moment. Gun fired, he moved aside to avoid but the bullet passed from rubbing his shoulder. The shock of the bullet caused him to fall down. Fortunately, an advertisement flex was hanging from the railing on which Vivek slid along and finally gripped its last end. Raghav ran away from there. Threatened by the sound of the shot, the general public was escaping from the mall to save their life. Everyone was in the first attempt to reach the gate.

Here Vivek was swinging between death hanging in the air.

Chapter seven

Facing off the death

* * *

Time : 1:20 pm. Afternoon.

"Leave the hand. We will catch you." There was the sound of the remnant. Scared people had already retired from the mall.

"Do not leave the hand. They are not going to catch you." It was the voice of Vivek's conscience, warning him.

Vivek in such circumstances had a firm belief in his tragic fate. The height was enough to break his bones. The sound of silence began to echo in his ears. The only thing he was able to listen at this moment was his heart beat, he could easily count them. His eyes unwillingly were looking down, seemed like the floor appeared as the bed of his death. Looking down to the floor, Vivek noticed a boy, wearing a blue check shirt was shooting his 'Khatron Ke Khiladi' video.

I am going to slap this boy hard if I safely reached to the floor. He vowed.

Sweat was tickling on his back. The stretching nerves were causing pain in the body. He was losing his grip due to growing sweat in the palm. The crowd and the floor began to blur. Then his eye fell on Amit coming to the second floor. He held the gun in his hand and pointed to Vivek. Vivek's eyes had been gone to Amit and his gun. He was looking at Amit's finger pushing back the trigger.

Dhak-dhak, dhak-dhak, dhak-dhak, dhak-dhak, dhak-dhak. Seeing this, his heartbeat started to match the speed of a train as the thought of Amit is going to kill him.

With a 'Dhany' sound bullet released out of the gun. Bullet hit a joint of flex which broke tying the rope from one side. Vivek's body was on the other side, waving. The lower border of flex hanging on the third floor was on the second floor. Flex reached the first floor because of the breaking rope. Vivek now comforting himself could jump. He left his hand and with a little shake reached to the floor safely.

As Vivek landed, the crowd rushed at him. Everybody asked his condition. Vivek cut the crowd.

A girl came straight to his chest. Surprised Vivek separated her from himself and saw her face.

"Sheena? You? What are you doing here?" by surprise, his voice was a little loud.

Sheena Pandey, Vivek's girlfriend, was standing in front of Vivek. Like a good love couple, dark skin colored Vivek had fair skin colored Sheena. White sleeveless top and blue jeans were praising her dressing sense. Her step cut long hair reached her back was extending her beauty. Sheena wore her beautiful ballet sandals two inches tall, which raised her height from five foot five inch to five foot seven inch, almost equal to Vivek's. She was a perfect looking girl.

"I came here with my friend for shopping." Her

friend was standing behind her. Vivek looked at her and shook his hand to say hi. Vivek had probably seen her in photographs.

"But how are you here? And why were you hanging there?" She asked while replying to Vivek.

Vivek replied. "Getting-up-there story, I will tell you later. First I have to complete two jobs...one minute."

Vivek reached to that boy wearing blue check shirt, who was still making his video. He slapped him very hard. Slapping noise reverberated, everybody trembled. On his cheeks were emerging Vivek's finger-prints. The boy boiled after the slap. Coming forward, he was about to answer Vivek back for his slap but he stopped and took his step back.

Vivek had seen the direction of his eyes which was looking behind the Vivek. Vivek Turned. Nikhil and Amit had come. The boy knew that Vivek might be harmful to his health. He gulped his anger, put his mobile in his pocket and left from there peacefully.

"This was the second. I'll see you, after settling the first important thing." Vivek tried to get rid of Sheena, but she was not going to give up so easily.

"What work? And is he your policemen friend Nikhil, isn't he?" She said, looking back to Nikhil. "Are you involved in some criminal activities?" Sheena started muttering.

"It's nothing like that yaar. Anything..."

"In that case, I'll come with you." Hearing her words Nikhil patted his forehead with his hands. Am-it's eyes then took a turn.

"Is there any movie is going on? Come on.. do your job." Scolded Nikhil. The people who were staring at them. They went on their on way.

"Sweetie! I'm not going to buy boots. The work that I am doing now is very dangerous. Our life is at stake." One more try from Vivek.

"I've seen so I will come with you for sure. The thought that I may lose you will haunt me, I will not sit peacefully." Sheena was very stubborn.

Vivek had once told Nikhil about it. Amit, Nikhil and Sheena's friend were looking at them. Of course, they did not want to get in between the crazy couple. Nikhil and Amit were hoping he could convince Sheena but they were wrong. Like every naive boyfriend, Vivek was not destined to win. The same happened this time. Sheena said while hugging Vivek. "Please take me with you. I will not disturb you. If I don't go. I will go crazy of fear. Please! Please! Please!"

Sheena's voice was a little saddened. She had used the girl's usual weapon, eye naivety and innocence of the face. Amit and Nikhil were seeing Vivek. Amit's and Nikhil's face had a clear gesture, saying do not say 'yes'.

"Yes!" Vivek said. Hearing that Amit turned back, Nikhil bowed his head and started moving to the right-left.

"Thank You, Thank You, Thank You!" Sheena woke tweet. He went to see off his friend.

Nikhil came to Vivek and said. "Are you mad? You said yes. Who knows how much further risk is there?"

"I know. But you don't know how much Khurafati, stubborn and dangerous she is?" Vivek said. They were whispering.

Nikhil asked with a puzzled expression. "Means?"

"As much as I know, if I would not take her with

us, she will secretly follow us. Don't you think she could take more risk like that?" Nikhil had remained speechless, listened to him. He understood the point of Vivek and had forced to agree to Vivek. Sheena was heading out with them now.

"What happened to doctor Chandraprakash?" Vivek asked.

Nikhil had desperation in the face. He answered with a blank face. "I followed him to 'Cross-word' and then my attention strayed to the sound of the shot. Then my eye had on you, you were hanging. I forgetting everything, ran at you. Amit luckily saved you."

The four went out of the mall went to their SUV's. Sheena was with Vivek.

Opening the door of the vehicle, asked Vivek. "Now where?"

"Dr.'s house." Nikhil went around to the other side of his vehicle and said. "Maybe we find him there."

"Now tell me what is going on?" Said Sheena sitting next to Vivek on the seat put his seatbelt.

"I'll tell you all." Vivek told her all about meeting Raghav to reaching to the mall. Their vehicles started running back to Nehru Nagar.

She sat like a little shocked to hear full particulars shall quote again, breaking his silence. "But how did you know that ...what was his name..." "Raghav."

"Yes, the killer is going to kill."

Vivek didn't tell Sheena about reading the mind. He removed part of his mind read by his story and the answer was already decided. He said. "His appearance and way of talking compelled me to think that he was telling the truth. And look! After moving on to follow him, I was proven right."

"Hmmm." Sheena's respond. Vivek and Sheena have reached Agrasen Chowk while talking.

"Oh My God!!!" Sheena blurted out. Front view shook her. She covered her mouth with her hand.

"Shit! Shit! Shit!" looking front direction, Vivek also got tongue-tied for a moment. He immediately increased the speed of his car. Amit and Nikhil's car went even faster. They saw Raghav pointing a gun at the doctor.

Bullet fired. Raghav killed one more in front of them. After shooting the doctor, he instantly went to him, quickly took something from his front pocket and ran out.

Chapter eight

Shock!

* * *

Time : 1:40 pm afternoon.

Both vehicles stopped at the scene. Vivek immediately came down and ran toward the doctor, Amit and Nikhil also got out from the vehicle and ran behind Raghav. Raghav killed the doctor on the roadside. He saw them, he ran in front of the traffic. Both ran to follow him, but unfortunately, he had already gone too far. Until the traffic reduced and they reached to the other side of the road, Raghav had escaped.

"Doctor! Doctor! Nothing will happen to you. We will take you to the hospital right now." Vivek said comforting Doctor. Sheena was calling ambulance back there.

Doctor's chest was soaked with blood. He was trying to say something to Vivek but Vivek wasn't able to understand, as the words are not clear. At the same moment, a black glimpse of visuals appeared to him. Even unintentionally, Vivek was reading his mind.

"Vivek!" Sheena's low voice broke Vivek's attention. He saw doctor's obligated neck on his lap. He had gone from the world. Vivek watched him with bound eyes. Sheena saw a murder first time in her life. Her eyes were overflowing with tears. With the voice of Nikhil's and Amit's returning footsteps, Vivek understood that they could not stop Raghav from escaping.

10 minutes later...

Ambulance and news channels were hungry for spicy news had reached there. News teams found some of those people who saw the accident near the road. They were trumpeting the failure of the police with love on the headlines. Nikhil ignored all the talk. He was giving the commissioner complete assessment of the situation over the phone. He was completing the formalities necessary for him to take over the case. Accompanying him, Amit was informing the situation to the Bilaspur police.

"What is happening there?" Watching Amit and Nikhil talking, Sheena asked Vivek.

"We'll know after going them." Vivek replied, pulling up his jacket sleeve. Nikhil, keeping Vivek's presence a secret had asked Vivek to stand a distance with Sheena.

Amit and Nikhil sidestepped the questions of the media, came out from there to Vivek. "Let's go back to the doctor's apartment. Perhaps we could find any clue from there. Here's just like the last member did not get anything other than a mobile without a SIM of his pocket." Nikhil told Vivek pushing his glasses to his nose.

Vivek opened the door of his vehicle and began to think of something. Nikhil's eyes were on him. "Vivek?" He called. Nikhil asked the question, only by calling his name.

Vivek, looking down, was lost in his thoughts. "Chest shot on a first one, and again only one bullet this time too..." "What are you talking to yourself?" Nikhil interrupted came to him and asked.

Vivek looked at Nikhil and in trembled tone he said. "He is going kill all four of them today and definitely today." Hearing this Nikhil got stunned. "How can you say that?" He asked.

"There...in the mall...he told me that he was going to spend four rounds of bullet today, here he spent only one bullet to each. Means..." Looking at Nikhil's face colour change, he realises that he need not say anything further. He remained silent.

Amit and Sheena were also listening to their conversation. "Come quickly." Nikhil told them both. The four sat on their vehicles. They were returning to Nehru Nagar.

Time: 02.05pm.

"Neighbours informed that this is flat." Reaching front door of a flat on the second floor, said Amit.

"Thankfully, at least one of the neighbors saw him, otherwise rest of them didn't even know that he had lived here." Said Nikhil eating cashews.

The door was locked. They asked for a hammer from a nearby neighbor and hacked the lock. All the four began to filter the rooms.

"Anything?" Nikhil asked Amit.

"No, sir!" Replied Amit. "Just the clothes - and got some books. Maybe we have to do some more digging."

"Find this." Vivek said interrupted between their

interactions. In his hand was a page which he directed toward them.

Nikhil came to him and said, to see the page. "Taj -Mahal and that's also slightly askew? What does it even mean?"

Vivek had just made that picture. Nikhil and Amit had understood what this was. Amit was trusting him too. "Find here something like Taj-Mahal. Painting or something." Vivek said.

Sheena, holding a novel like a fool which she lifted from the table front of her, was standing there watching everything. She could not understand this. She came to him and said, staring at Vivek. "Why have you made this. And why is everybody looking for it?" She looked, taking the novel into her hand and said.

"Now don't say that you don't know about Vivek's abilities about reading minds of a person just by touching them." Amit said with his well-known seriousness and sense of rudeness.

"What??" Sheena's face became like her father fixed her marriage without telling. His eyes went bigger.

"Shucks you!!" Vivek drubbed his forehead. "Why do you think we are taking the matter seriously enough. Thanks to him we have reached these people who are living here, changing their identity." Telling this, Nikhil contributed in Vivek's forehead drubbing.

"It means...it means..." Sheena's face was worth watching. Her eyes started twirling around them, first Nikhil then Amit and finally froze on Vivek. "...You were telling the truth that day." Sheena's tongue stuck on the whole thing.

"Yeeesss!!" Vivek looked up his head and answered by dragging the words.

Sheena taking dives in the ocean of surprises came to Vivek and said blazed. Therefore I wondered that who is the boyfriend born in this world who fulfills all wishes of her girlfriend that she just thought and didn't even tell him."

Nikhil and Amit who were yet standing surprised at the response of Sheena now understood what the matter was. "So...you did not tell her yet?" Said Nikhil.

"No!!" Sheena answered instead of Vivek in anger.

"I told her...in the first meeting, but she took it as a joke. Since then, I thought not telling her would be best."

"But...I'll not let this go. I hate you!" Sheena erupted in anger threw that novel on him which she held in her hand.

Vivek caught the book in the hands. Catching the book, Vivek's eyes fell on the slip dropped on the floor from inside the novel. He picked it up, and by seeing it put it back in the novel. "Throwing book like this is not good..." Vivek suddenly stopped speaking. He immediately opened the book again. And quickly began to turn its pages. Nikhil and Sheena saw his desperate struggle and come to him.

"What happened? What have you seen that you keep looking?" Nikhil said.

"Look at this!" Vivek showed Nikhil an open page of that novel.

Nikhil took it on his hands and went to Sheena, took a page out of his hand.

"What happened to you two?" Sheena asked.

Nikhil did not respond. Looking to the novel, he put that page on the table and begun to write some-thing with his pen. He started writing by rolling over every page carefully.

'Heart'. He wrote down, turned few pages. A circle marked on page number of a page. '36' he wrote. 'Heartland' and 'Narayana' he wrote down further. After filtering the entire novel found a temple-sketch drawn on the last page. Beneath the temple, '430P' was written.

"Heart, 36, Gadh, Narayan, 430P and the temple symbol-painting." Sheena curiously and seriously said. "What does this mean?"

A few words on the novel were circling. Nikhil uncovered the words from the whole novel. Now they seem to understand the meaning of those words. After searching the entire room disappointed Amit joined them. Scratching his head for ten minutes Nikhil replied. "It means Janjgir - Champa district Vish-nu - Temple, four-thirty in the evening."

"How can you say that?" Sheena questioned.

Nikhil round up first three words together to the circular, said. "Heart, thirty-six and Gadh...means Heart of Chhattisgarh' what 'Janjgir - Cham-pa' district is called."

Vivek also understood the matter. He said finishing Nikhil's sentence. "..And Narayan means Lord Vishnu."

Sheena said further. "Oh! The last Temple figure means Vishnu Temple."

"Yes! And time is mentioned in last."

The 'P' means 'pm."' Said Nikhil.

"So are they gonna be there?" Amit said. "Maybe it is possible that doctor was going to meet with the members there?"

"No! not there." Vivek broke their assumptions.
"Why?" All spoke together.

Vivek showed the bill of the novel and said. "Look at this! Because this place was set a few months ago from today." The bill had been purchased on the date of the last month. "Today they were supposed to meet somewhere else."

Nikhil looked at Amit with hopes. Amit shook his head in 'no'.

Amit searched the corners of the rooms. Like last time he did not find anything this time too. Nikhil while caressing his head with fingers, sat down on the chair was placed there. Tension again kicked out the bad poet inside Nikhil.

"kambakht maut bhi kitni zaalim nikli, jaan to li hi raaz bhi dafan kar gayi."

"I do not know what does the Taj-mahal mean." Vivek said. While both his hands behind on television placed on the table and looked up his head. Two minutes all remained quiet. The sudden flashes in mind of Vivek. He stood upright in shock and asked Nikhil. "Where you saw him last time at the mall?"

"Cross...Word !! Oh yes!" Nikhil stood up happily and got out of the room. All three ran after him.

"What happened? What has been discovered?" Sheena asked maintaining her speed with Vivek's speed.
"The Novel shop name on the bill is written crossword and doctor entered Crossword last time. This means he went there to know next location." Vivek replied.

They all reached down and sat in their vehicles. Their vehicles were heading back to Magneto Mall.

Vivek was able to sense outrage of Sheena by seeing her face bloated. He tried to persuade her. "So you did not believe me what can I do?" He said.

"Will you listen to me for once?" Sheena softly spoke with the serious tone.

"For what?"

She said turning her face toward his. "Get out of this case."

"What...What are you saying?" It confused Vivek.

"I'm not getting a right feeling about all this." Her face reflected a clear sense of discomfort and anxiety.

"I have two policemen with me. Do not worry." "That is why I'm worrying." "What are you...?"

"You probably do not understand it. As you have told me that, I'm afraid. Think Otherwise...whose lives are at stake instead of seeking for a help of police they are running away from them." Sheena was referring that restaurant situation.

"Yes! But the doctor didn't know that."

"You said that doctor ignored Amit in the restaurant even when he was in uniform. And by the way, they all, left everything are staying here means that it must be a very big case." Sheena forced him to think. In this whole thing, till now, He did not look into this aspect of the situation.

Sheena added. "Who knows how many powerful persons are involved in all this. You just got involved coincidently in all this." Sheena said lovingly put his hand on her shoulder. "If you jumped into the wrong war then should rectify the mistake by leaving to see the right time at the war."

Sheena had shaken Vivek's mind, silently and speechless, he was driving now. He wanted to say something. By saying anything he wanted to prove Sheena wrong but a part of his mind had acknowledged that this was true. Then his phone began to vibrate.

"Commissioner Sir?" Reading out the name of the caller on the mobile screen, Vivek started.

"Do you have commissioner's number?"

"No... And I had not even put my phone in silent and vibration mode, wait..." Vivek Suddenly remembered something. "...Will surely Amit's. We have the similar set, therefore, we must have picked up the wrong set".

"Pick up the phone and tell him." Sheena said. To agree with Sheena, Vivek attended the call. "Hel-lo!!" He said.

"Hello! Why did you not report to me yet." From the other side, even before Vivek could say anything the Commissioner had begun. "Keep an eye on that Vivek guy, if he wouldn't do anything wrong and keep reporting me the whole thing."

Hearing about himself from Commissioner, Vivek stunned. "Amit? What happened? Why aren't you saying anything? Are Vivek and Nikhil there?"

Vivek personally handled promptly and respond by mimicking the sounds of Amit. "They are...yes!"

"Well! I will wait for your reports." So saying, the commissioner disconnected the phone.

Sheena asked. "What happened? What did he say?"

"Nothing. The voice was not audible clearly." Vivek hides the talk and removed his number from call history. Sheena already was bothered by his involvement in the case. He did not want to bother her more. Sheena was feeling the silence of Vivek but she was unaware of the real thing. This was a dilemma to Vivek because back at the mall, Amit had just saved his life.

Chapter nine

Inclined Taj Mahal

* * *

Time : 2:30 pm afternoon.

They arrived at the mall.

Sheena said before getting out from the vehicle. "You just tell them that you do not want to remain involved in all this."

So saying, Sheena was opening the door off, holding her hand Vivek said. "I've decided Sheena. I will not separate myself from the case." Sheena to hear Vivek's decision she wanted to say something further but holding up her, Vivek continued. "And yes... I'm sprung, even by mistake in this war but I'm stern of this war now. And anyway, I believe there's no such thing as coincidence. It is the time that decides everyone's part and put them together in its own way."

God knows which kind of magic those words did to Sheena, she didn't say anything more and understood that Vivek is not going to be stepping back.

Four got out from the vehicles. Bilaspur police had come and had engaged in the proceedings. Nikhil gestured three to come inside after talking necessary things with the police. Seeing Sheena and Vivek with Nikhil, others raised no objection.

"Here's your phone." Vivek extended Amit's mobile towards him. "Our sets were exchanged at the mall."

Amit saw his set and then saw Vivek. Amit thanked him. While Amit was taking mobile, Vivek recognized nervousness on his face. Vivek had already removed Commissioner's number from mobile calls list from Amit's mobile.

"Anyone...did anyone call?" Amit asked hesitating.

Sheena standing behind Vivek was about to open her mouth to answer, without being seen by anyone Vivek grabbed her hand firmly. "No! Nobody." Vivek replied. Sheena was looking at Vivek questioning.

Amit pushed forward with Nikhil. The focus of Vivek was now on the Amit.

They all entered quickly and headed to crossword. Some police officers were talking to people in a costly suit. Richness and botheration were evident on their face. They were three. One of them was a young boy who was more tetchy to the officer standing in front of them. Was not hard to guess where they were the owners of the mall and pressing on officers to resolve the incident as quickly as possible.

Seeing Nikhil saluted by his juniors. "Do not forget to ask them how the gun sneaked inside by the guilty even after the existence of metal detector. What was their security doing?" Nikhil said. Saying this, he raised a question on the Mall Authority. Nikhil stared at the boy. His mouth got shut and eyes tipped.

The four arrived at the crossword book shop. The shop was open. Obviously, they didn't have the time to lock shop during the stampede.

"Now what? How to find the book in the whole shop. Thousands of books are here." Sheena said, giving a look to the books. Sheena had raised questions about an important thing which nobody thought yet. They had sailed into another dilemma.

Their mind began to wander again. After thinking for a while Vivek remembered something. He said. "Do not have to look at all. Search for this, anything like Taj Mahal."

Now they understood what could have been the reason of visual of Taj Mahal on doctor's mind read by Vivek. All of them had divided the shelves among them to find the book. Amit was looking in thriller novels section. Beside him was the historical books section where Vivek was looking for. Sheena and Nikhil were in the sections of Love Stories and Indian Mythology respectively.

"Got it. Got it." Sheena shouted. In her hand was a novel. She came to Vivek. Vivek asked Sheena for that page and began matching with the picture that he made. Both were the same. Slant Taj Mahal, which bound with chains.

"Like the previous one, this is also a love story based novel." Sheena said.

They found the book. Down on the floor of that section, the new edition of this book was arranged near the shelf in a systematic manner, one over another. They all explored the whole books together.

"It is nothing....No handwriting and no marking." Disappointed Nikhil spoke slowly while throwing last copy on the shelf.

A beautiful sofa was placed in front for the readers. Vivek sat there. Sheena came and sat next to him with putting elbows of her both hands on knee and palms on the face.

"Time is passing quickly. We are looking for the next place here where he will probably kill them." Vivek said frustrated.

Nikhil came to him and said. "Do not worry! We'll find that scientist and reach before Raghav." Nikhil heartened Vivek.

"I trust you..." Before completing the sentence, Nikhil's mobile began to vibrate. He took out the mobile and irritated, seeing the screen. "She is still on sorry... now, who will explain her situation here is so bad that wc didn't even eat food yet."

"Payal?" Vivek assumed.

Shaking his head 'yes' Nikhil on his mobile sent her a message. He was irritated.

Definitely didn't send a love message. Vivek surmised.

Vivek was gazing at the arrangement of the new version of that book as was not able to think of any idea. That time, his childhood memories started flashing into his mind when his father started his teaching sessions. It was just two days later when Vivek was twelve years old and just learned about his extraordinary abilities.

"Oooooom." Mr. Devesh pronounced.

"Oooooom." Vivek pronounced with him.

6 O'clock in the morning, they both were sitting on a mat, legs bent in the yoga position, at the garden of the home, fresh air of atmosphere was cooling their bodies and comforting mind, peace all around with delightful fragrances, the absence of unpleasant noise and no other distractions. Everything was making it the best time for meditation.

They were sitting in the small garden of their beautiful house. There were trees all around covering that area.

"I saved Bua from that cheap fellow two days ago." Eyes opened, 12-year-old Vivek said, turning his head towards his dad. "I thought you will give me something but we are doing this instead." He added.

"How can I give somebody something who is gifted by nature." Devesh responded, opened his eyes. Vivek didn't understand actual meaning behind this line. He kept looking at him. Devesh also turned his head towards Vivek.

"What do you think about dreams?" Asked Devesh.

"Dreams are dreams. What about them?" Vivek answered shrugging.

Devesh smiled at his answer and said. "They are not just dreams son. Sometimes they show us what had happened in past, what is going in the present and what is going to happen in future."

"What??" This was the reaction Devesh expected from a boy who possibly experienced the dream as bad and good.

"I strongly believe in that. Therefore I bought you here with me to teach something you should learn." Devesh said.

"How and why papa? What have you seen in your dream?" Vivek said anxiously.

"I..." Devesh spoke, gazing at Vivek, he stopped for a moment and then continued. "...I saw you fell in a pit surrounded by some three or I think four people, laughing at you. You were obligated, shouting for help and the worst thing was..."

"What??" Vivek interrupted. His face was evidencing that Devesh totally extended Vivek's interest in this.

"...You were calling them for help with their name. It was like you knew them. Like they were your friends." Devesh ended all talking.

"Then....??" Watching him quiet for few moments, asked Vivek.

"Then...I woke up."

Vivek remained silent.

Devesh sensed the fear in Vivek. He put his hand on Vivek's shoulder, smiled and said. "I was not there but I am here now." He continued. " Giving skills to us is God's part. But learning and taking control is upon us. This is the part we have to do on our own. This mind reading thing, you must have to learn to use it. From now on, you will wake up with me and do yoga with me for next two months."

"How's this yoga gonna work for me?"

"Yoga is very effective my son. As you know, you started sweating and shaking hands when this visions appeared to you."

"So?"

"So, yoga will help you to concentrate and soothe your senses. You must conquer this problem. These are controlling you but you have to control them."

"And after two months?" Vivek questioned. Devesh looked at him for a moment and turned his head back to position. Closed his eyes and began to chanting 'OM' again.

Two months later...

"What is this papa? I can't do it like this." Said Vivek.

"But you have to." Devesh forced him.

It Was 10 O' clock in the morning. There was a road passing through their home satiated with vehicles, noisy sounds and distractions. Fresh air was replaced with exhausting smokes from vehicles, peace with horns. The garden was the only one thing which hadn't changed. It was the worst time for meditation. Vivek didn't want to do this in this unpleasant atmosphere but his father kept forcing him.

"Why?? Why do you want me to do this?" Vivek asked in a harsh way.

"Because I want you to be prepared for every situation. Concentrating in a suitable environment is very easy but in a disturbing situation like this is tough."

"But...." Irritated Vivek tried to say something but his father stopped him and gestured him to sit on the mat. He couldn't argue more with his father, therefore, he had to sit.

Watching his unwillingness, Devesh explained him in a soft tone. "Listen, son, maybe you find this all unfavorable. But I believe that you have come here to do something big. Great skills also took great troubles. When you will step in trouble, this is gonna help in some way."

Vivek slightly understood his means. He closed his eyes and chanted 'OM'.

Days were passing and Vivek was getting better with his senses.

After one month, sweating was no longer a problem now, but he had still some issues with hands shuddering. They both were on the roof in the morning at 10 O' clock. It was empty. Only those two were there. Vivek was sitting on a chair had a pencil on his hand, was looking prepared to draw something on that page which was placed on the table in front of him.

"You have impressed me son. Now we'll go further." Said Devesh. "In past thirty days as we know that your biggest problem is your uncontrolled hand. Starting from today we will be focusing on that problem." Devesh put his hand on Vivek's shoulder and said. "Try to see something."

It was very important for Vivek to cure that problem. He wanted to do it very badly. After touching him, Devesh's mind plans appeared to Vivek. Like always, his hands began shuddering in a pattern as they are trying to do something.

"Do it." Devesh shouted. His voice automatically raised in this moment.

Vivek immediately started sketching something on the page. Meanwhile, Devesh was looking at his watch. It took several minutes to complete the sketch.

"Me going for a bath, not bad." Said Devesh chuckling.

"Yeah! I draw a pretty good picture of you." Vivek chuckled too.

"Not picture, I meant timing. This time you finished it just in fifteen minutes."

"You mean to say..."

"Yes." Devesh confirmed.

Signs were clear. Meditation was helping him not only to control and use that powers but to getting better at it in terms of time. Day by day practice was making him better.

Devesh said. "It'll improve more." Vivek shook his head in response.

Ambling around Vivek, Devesh added in a very deep tone. "When life comes at a risk, people's minds work in two ways. Either it starts to work fast or stop completely. I pray to God not to come that day in your life, but if it happens, you have to run your mind like a train. As I told you, trouble occurs according to skills and your skills are extraordinary. If you know what I mean. Having talent is not big of a deal but using them in right time is." His strong and inspiring voice was encountering in Vivek's mind.

"I understand papa." Said Vivek in a serious tone.

"Now, close your eyes, concentrate on visuals

and start drawing. I want you to ignore this all distractions like they are not even existing."

Vivek did the same. He was so good at this now that at this time he was not even listening to his father's voice.

Dhak-dhak,dhak-dhak,dhak-dhak.

He was even able to listen to his heartbeats clearly.

Days passed. Vivek was improving day by day. Thirty minutes of drawing became fifteen and then became ten.

After six months of meditation and teaching session of Devesh, Vivek was now able to complete a sketch just in a minute. Vivek vowed to bring it to seconds.

Thinking about his father's lessons, Vivek closed his eyes and started concentrating. After two minutes he suddenly stood up as if he found something.

"What happened?" Sheena and Nikhil said together. Vivek said. "All copies were well stacked. Why will doctor arrange that book back during trouble time after reading it?"

Amit immediately understood Vivek's intention. "You want to say that..." He bowed down to the knees and began to look remaining gaps un-der the shelf. "...That The book, probably, would have been thrown somewhere here."

"There is no harm in looking." Vivek said. Hearing his voice, Nikhil and Sheena also began to see the floor.

"Got it." Amit's voice reverberated throughout the hall. He got up from his place and said, while the finger pointing towards the third bookshelf.

The shelf was arranged one after another in a queue. "There." Declaring, Amit immediately went to the third self. He stooped down, picked up the book and turning its pages came to it.

"Secrets are never buried. Their nature is to tearing out the grave." Vivek quipped that poetry of the Nikhil as per the situation.

Nikhil looked at him, smiling and took over the book and began to rinse the pages. Vivek took that page back in his hand. A copy of the book was in his hand. He and Nikhil sat down on the same couch. Nikhil started finding words. As soon as he sees a marked word, he says and Vivek used to write it on the page. Ten minutes later in front of them, had a whole series of words to distinguish the address.

"Bowl, photographers, Smile, Heart Paddy, 500 and evening." Vivek read. "The last time it was easier."

"It is five o'clock in the evening time for sure." Amit took the pen out of the hand of Vivek and cut '500' and 'Evening'.

"Everybody understood that." Sheena said teasing Amit.

"This place is again Champa in Chhattisgarh." Amit said. Eyes filled with question, watching Amit, Vivek asked him. "How can you say that?"

Amit cut bowl and Paddy in response and said. "Bowl means 'Katora' also and paddy means 'Dhaan'. It means 'Dhaan ka Katora'."

"Which is the CHHATTISGARH state." Nikhil exclaimed immediately. "Yes!" cutting Heart, said Amit. "This time also 'heart' means 'Dil' means 'Janjgir-Champa.'"

"This is fine enough. But the smile and the photographer remain left." Vivek said pointing continuously his finger on those two words. "Probably, he is a photographer who smiles more." Sheena on her estimated.

"Now how will we find such type of per-son?" Vivek said. Picking and said Nikhil. "Let's go there, then we decide our next step." Nikhil eye gestured Amit.

Amit took the hint and immediately said, standing straight. "We will be there in one and a half hour, sir!"

"Wondering how Dr. cracked the codes in such rush?" Sheena asked while they were in the lift going to ground floor.

"Page number pattern," answered Vivek. "like first one, this novel had marked words on same pages.".

Chapter ten

First meeting of love

* * *

5 months ago from today. August 2015. Bilaspur.

The pub, where people drink with their friends enjoy the music and dance. Somewhere a group of girls and boys were enjoying, love couples were having fun somewhere. A place, where youth drank with all the exhaustion and rush of the life dissolved in wine bottles. Saturday evening, they wait for this evening the most. Sunday is the day of the holiday; therefore no other day could be better for having late night fun. Some people were on the dance floor dancing to the beat of the music, while some were sitting, just participating by moving their necks and legs on the beat.

Here somewhere, Sheena was sitting alone in the corner. "One More." She finished his last glass of vodka and the said to the bartender, pointing. He gave Sheena her next drink. Vivek came and sat right next to her by showing two fingers pointed towards the bartender.

Bilaspur, two years ago, he used to live here. He used to come here often, therefore, he became a known customer and had a good rapport with the bartender. Vivek lifted and drank the peg, without look-ing to Sheena, said. "Too much drinking is injurious to health."

He glued her the warning advertisement from theatres before the movie starts.

Sheena turned right side towards him, watching in a funny way said. "Who are you? And it's none of you business that how much I drink?" Sheena replied fretfully. She was speaking words, dragging on the tongue. Perhaps it was the effect of alcohol intoxication. Vivek smiled slightly. He had expected her to respond like that.

He again smiled and said. "I know the break-up is very painful. I'm just going through the same situation." Vivek took a shot and said.

"Pain?..." Sheena had a hiccup with a grin and said in drunken style. "...Who the hell is drinking to forget the pain? I am drinking so I can digest happiness." So saying, Sheena swallowed the whole peg. "But how did you know?"

"Right here, my laptop password just dumped me."

"Was she hot?"

"Yeah!! Very."

"So Sad. What was the problem?"

"Leave it, what will you do...It's a long long story."

10 minutes later.

"It's a very very sad story of yours.... too bad." Said Sheena stomping a glass on the table, she just finished one more peg. Vivek pulled his lower lip a little further ahead and shook his head, said. "Hmmm." "Well, tell me something. How did you know that she is cheating on you?"

"Ahamm." Vivek cleared his throat and said. "I will not tell a lie to you. Actually, I read her mind."

"Whatttt?" Sheena responded surprisingly. "Yeah! You heard that right, I can read mind just by a touch."

Listening to Vivek, Sheena stared at him for two moments. Then immediately started laughing out loud. They got attention from people around them. Vivek began to look around. He started to feel like a fool. Vivek understood his goodness to say nothing.

"One more peg here." Sheena was raising her hand to order when Vivek, grabbing her hand, stopped her. You have had enough." Vivek said.

"Enough?...you are a fucking blot in name of men. You have just finished four pegs yet. See...I made a line of wine here." Her style was like a stoned one but the voice was reflecting naivety and childishness. "And look.. still..I can stand straight..." She got up from the chair and fell onto the floor with the sound of 'Dhamma'.

People around started staring at them again. Vivek saw Sheena first with torn eyes and open mouth and then people.

"Hey, get up. What happened to 'Amitabh Bachchan from Sharaabi'?" Vivek with the great difficulties lifted her up. Her purse was in her left hand, which was lying on the floor because of her fall. Vivek rummaged her purse and then picked out of her mobile phone from that.

"Shit!! pin password!" Vivek put the phone back in the purse, It proved rubbish for him. Jammed purse in one hand and his other hand was giving sup-port her to move forward. Some people were still staring at them.

Sheena was bubbling across the way while Vivek

was taking her home. In such a case he had not any choice. Thankfully, he was less drunk compared to her. Vivek brought her to his uncle's flat. His uncle was away for a few days and Vivek had come here for a few days.

"Why do people become heavy after drinking?" He whispered to himself. Lifting Sheena with both hands, He was forwarding ahead. The flat was on the second floor. After reaching the lift he stepped to the door of his flat, which was right in front of the elevator. He took her there carefully. Her purse had left no stone unturned to tease Vivek like it was taking some kind of revenge of previous life. It frequently often slipping off down from the shoulder of Vivek. He was about to open the door of his apartment. Just then Mr. Khanna, his uncle's neighbour came out from his apartment.

"Why is he staring at me as if I have lifted HIS daughter?"

Mr. Khanna slipped from beside him, staring. Vivek saw him peek and opened the door, entered straightway inside. She had stopped her bubbling. She was already unconscious. Vivek brought her to his room and laid her on the bed.

After covering her with a sheet, Vivek was about to go when Sheena grabbed his hand. She pulled him to the bed and brought her face very close to the face of Vivek.

"What the..." Vivek astonished by the act of Sheena, tried to say something. Putting a finger on his lips, Sheena made him quiet by generating the sound 'Sshshshsshshsh...' loudly. Vivek got quiet. Sheena's intoxicating eyes were looking to his eyes.

"Are you..hitch...gonna cheat on me like him?" Sheena's eyes were delirious and her tongue was stumbling. The body was tired. She did not know what she was saying. This question was indicating Sheena's pain which she tried to hide and the fact that she's over his cheater ex-boyfriend. Vivek can see her sadness in her eyes clearly.

Vivek smiled slightly at first, then said, noting with eyes full of love. "No. Never."

As Sheena heard this, she smiled spreading her lips on either side of the face and fell on the bed. Vivek kept watching her. Sometime later Vivek took off her heels. He laid down covering himself a sheet on a three seater sofa which was there in front of the bed. His eyes were still gazing at her pretty face. He began to enjoy the innocence of her sleeping face.

While watching her, he began to think about his step that if he had decided to go back home with his friends, he never got a chance to see Sheena like this. He was chatting with his friend sitting and finishing beer bottle when his eye went on Sheena. Both anger and tears were visible on her face. She was shouting at somebody. He didn't know who ... It could not even matter to Vivek. He was just looking at her.

His friend asked him to go back. But he refused by making excuses. Now, there was a boy among them. This was the same boy she was yelling. After a while, he got out of there. Now there was no one between the two. Sheena started to drink. Vivek saw her for a while but now he did not want to lose the chance to talk to her. He sat down beside her and began to speak, making a fictitious story about girlfriend break-up.

Now he was happy for this. Seeing Sheena, when he slept, he didn't even know.

His ears heard a sound. 'Tak-tak' of heels, his

eyes opened slowly. Seven hours had passed, It was morning already. He saw that Sheena was searching for something, looking around. Her sight stopped in front of the television, she went there and picked up her purse. She was gonna go then she saw that Vivek has woke-up and watching her.

Vivek stood. "Thank You!" Sheena came near, looked at him and said. Then she began to leave.

"Let me drop you." Vivek said. Sheena permitted, the two from here climbed the first step of love called friendship.

Chapter eleven

Smart One

* * *

Time : evening 4:30 pm today.

Both vehicles had entered Janjgir-Champa district exhausting smoke. Meanwhile, Amit had asked Nikhil the story of the unfolding of Vivek's extraordinary and secret skill to him. Nikhil didn't have any reason not to tell him this time. He told him everything.

"That day he didn't make a picture?" Hearing the whole story, asked Amit.

"I also asked him when he told me that he also drew images, he said he did not need it that time. A bit of a thought appeared in the mind of those boys because of the fear, after looking me was enough to identify them."

"Oh! In our case it is very important to understand everything, therefore he also made sketches." Amit said. Nikhil nodded his head agreeing and said. "Right, Nayak! I asked him how long it takes him to read anyone's mind but he avoided."

Here Sheena was still discussing a very important matter with Vivek. "I still did not understand why you did not tell Amit about commissioner's phone call?"

"Be...Because even I did not properly understand what he said." Vivek replied, trying to escape from the question. “I am not thinking about that right now. The most important things are to understand ‘Smile’ and ‘photographer.’”

While talking, Vivek saw Amit’s vehicle was stopped ahead. Amit was asking something from some guy on the street.

“Call Nikhil.” Vivek said to Sheena.

Sheena immediately called Nikhil and put the phone on speaker.

Nikhil picked up the phone and Vivek started talking to him. “What happened? What did you ask the guy?”

Nikhil replied. “Nothing was coming on my mind so I thought to ask about the photographer who laughs.”

“Found anything?”

“No! The man stared us in a funny way but we must keep our eyes open.Stop! Stop!” Nikhil shouted. Their vehicles were about to move. Suddenly Nikhil’s sight fell on something and he asked Amit to reverse the vehicle. “Reverse! Reverse!” Amit slightly reversed the vehicle.

Vivek overheard his talking through the speaker. He stopped his vehicle and landed with Sheena. “Why did you stop…” Before he could complete, a board on front answered his question.

“Muskaan photo studio! Second-floor shop number thirty-three!” Sheena also read the name on the board.

The board was on the wall outside the complex. On the board was a portrait of a smile, the emoticon. The emoticon had placed the camera in hand. “Let’s take a chance to this also.” Said Nikhil came forward. “Let’s go!”

They all went to the second floor.

It was a two-story complex, which was situated aligned with another shop and placed in a fine line with the queue of a complex. 'Krishna' was written on the complex's name board. To reach the ground floor, five stairs had to be climbed. There was a passage straight from the stairs which was going forward. On both sides of the passage, shops were open. Some of the shops were still not rented.

"That's the lift!" Vivek said.

There was a passage from the right side of the path, was ended on a lift. They moved in the elevator. The elevator was going up. On the right there were stairs. The decrepitude of walls along the stairs was reflecting the decline in maintenance. Amit, after reaching near the elevator pressed the button to open the elevator.

Maybe in keeping me alive, he has some benefit. But he has Nikhil's trust and I don't have any strong evidence. To assure Nikhil I have to read his mind to identify what the hell he is doing?

The door of the lift opened and thinking of his next move, Vivek decided. Amit had come under the cloud of Vivek now. Amit had raised a question in Vivek's mind which could be answered only by reading Amit's mind. They all stepped inside the elevator. Amit, Nikhil were ahead, Vivek and Sheena were behind them. Vivek was looking at Amit. In a few seconds, they were to reach the second floor.

"It will not be a better time to read his mind." Vivek had prepared him for an effrontery step.

He raised his hand and began to take it to his shoulder. His hand almost reached Amit's shoulder. Amit instantly turned back. Vivek immediately lowered his arm.

"What happened?" Amit asked.

Vivek was a little bit nervous, his nervousness appeared on his forehead as a sweet blob. "Nothing! Just nothing!" Vivek completely tried to hide his nervousness.

They reached the second floor. The door opened and the four went out.

"Shit!!" A good chance slipped from Vivek's hand.

They were going by counting the number of stores. They crossed a book and mobile stores and came to the 'Muskan studio'. In front was a counter, a nearly thirty-year-old man was sitting. He was doing some calculations on the counter and opened a register.

"Now what??" Vivek Saw Nikhil and asked. "Do we wait here?"

"Both the times it was Champa which means that it is clear that whoever is next, lives here. Maybe he knows about him."

Going forward, said Amit. "Let's ask." He went to the man. "Do you recognize him?" Amit showed him an original picture of Dr. Chandraprakash and asked about the two scientists survivors.

"Straight to the point! He does not have to waste time at all." Thoughts came to Vivek's mind.

The man carefully saw the photograph and said. "No! Not that I remember."

Amit drew out doctor Chandraprakash's picture from his pocket and showed him that picture which he had clicked after his death. "Look carefully." It was doctor's fake getup photo.

The man looked at that and said. "Oh yes!! He had come here." He said by rubbing both sides of his eyes.

Their guess hit right on the target. Listening to him, Nikhil and Vivek came to him and Vivek asked. "Mr. ...?"

"Charan Saagar."

"Mister Charan! When did they come?"

"Now I do not remember much, but ... Yes! It must have been fifteen to thirteen days. Why?? Is he sick?" He estimated the man by closed eyes on the picture.

"No! He is dead." Amit said in a serious voice. Charan's eyes spread. His entire mood evaporated.

Nikhil said. "Did somebody come with him?"

Listening to the question of Nikhil, Charan seemed to remember something. "Yes! A bhaisaheb came with him."

"Do you know him?"

"No... not! But I will recognize him. One day on my way home, I saw his house. Looked like this gentleman." He pointed to doctor David from group photo who kept a test tube at the left hand.

Nikhil saw a silver lining. He explained to him. "Look! Today he may probably came here. We will be there at the neighborhood shop. If he comes, nod at me. Understood?"

"For sure!" He nodded his head and said.

Vivek and Amit entered the book store after two stores. Here there were two computers also on which the boys were surfing the internet. It was an internet hub too. Vivek's eyes were on the computer screen. An on-line application was being filled. A twenty-year-old boy sitting in front of the screen was operating the computer. Nearly five years older than him, a boy was sitting next to him. He was telling the boy some important things, according to which the kid was filling in the application.

"How can I help you?" A fat dark skin colored man came to both and asked. His fat tummy, short height, oil-stained hair, face and the entire appearance were putting him in a usual boring man category.

Vivek looked at the stationary items behind him and replied, thinking. "Um... do you have comic books?"

The man first gazed at him as response and said. "No. We don't have. Who read comic books these days?" Amit gazed at Vivek too.

"I read." He said. Now he hadn't anything to ask for. He rotated his eyes towards Amit as a hint. Now Amit had to aim with the bow and arrow.

Sheena and Nikhil from the left-hand side of the photo studio entered a gift store. There was one more queue from this shop. Nikhil had frozen his eyes on the studio. According to the clues, the next member should've come by 5 O'clock.

"How much??" Sheena asked shopkeeper. She had a brown colored teddy bear on her hand. She took it to counter.

Thick frame spectacles wearing shopkeeper, 'Pakoda' nose mounted on the face tipped the teddy, looked at the price tag and said. "500 bucks." His nose was thick and big that feels like his nose must enter the door before him.

"What? Five hundred?" Her voice automatically raised. Starting bargain, She said. "In Bilaspur, it would have not more than three hundred bucks." And she aggravated the war.

He struck back. "No ma'am, look at that, how beautiful is it? And the quality, touch it yourself." He let her show by pressing the teddy and handed to her.

Nikhil sure had an eye on the studio from there but he also had his ears on what Sheena was saying. It was deteriorating his mind, but she was making it easy for Nikhil. For the shopkeeper, they were a couple. Nikhil's dalliance made the shopkeeper think that he was a frustrated boyfriend with a hot and chatty girlfriend, who could not let her go and had to put up with her shopping tantrums.

On the other hand, Amit and Vivek here were still thinking of how to pass time. So now they had the stroll after walking out of the store. They were kicked out from a store for not buying anything. Not having a girl became a cause of botheration. They both almost excursed all other stores there. Sheena's one negotiation segment was longer than the circumambulation of the two. Compulsively they had to start strolling. Vivek was thinking of getting the chance to read Amit's mind as well. As they were walking back and forth, he couldn't get it.

Time: 5.30 pm.

Vivek's eye fell on Nikhil while strolling. He was heading to a studio after coming out of the store. Sheena was coming behind. He was tired of waiting. Only a woman came to photographed. Amit and Vivek were forced back to the studio. Nikhil went to Charan, said. "Do you know the phiz of the man?"

"Yes!" He said.

"So...Why didn't you tell me?" Nikhil flared on him.

"You never asked." Charan replied naively. "I'll write you his address." He tore a page behind the register.

He drew a few lines and gave them a place name.

"Thank you!" Amit said took the page. At the same time, Vivek moved his hand to take the page. Both hand-touched and separated from each other.

"Sorry!" Vivek said. *Shit! Missed again.*

Nikhil and Sheena were moving ahead, Amit and Vivek were trailing.

A twenty-year-old boy came out from the same bookstore holding some papers in the hand. He was the same boy who was filling up the online forms. Amit saw him and said to Vivek. "You go, I'm coming." Vivek nodded his head and moved forward.

Sheena and Nikhil had reached the elevator. Vivek gestured them to go. He turned right to catch the stairs. Sheena and Nikhil had entered into the lift. The elevator door closed. Vivek went ahead but did not down. He took his steps back and stuck his ear to the wall and tried to listen to the conversation of Amit to that boy's.

"What are you doing here Nitin?"

"I'm doing the thing you said to do." Nitin said to him shaking his papers.

"There should be no mistake like the last time. Otherwise, I'll break your rotten old laptop and this time there will be more than one day in jail." Intimidated Amit. Nitin nodded his head in 'Yes' and Amit began to move, showing him his deadly eyes.

From the sound of his footsteps, Vivek was alerted and went running up the stairs. He crossed four steps taking long jumps. Similarly, by jumping all the way he scaled down and before arriving down he maintained himself. He gasped his all exhaustion by standing there.

Amit scaled down. "Still here?" He said look-ing

at Vivek.

"Yup! I have been waiting for you. Let's go." Vivek was trying hard not to gasp and he probably did it. Amit looked at Vivek from down to the top and then went ahead without a word.

Amit crossed Vivek, matching his speed and at the same time whispered in his ears. "Reading my mind is not that easy." Vivek got stunned and kept watching Amit go.

I *have to do something. I have to do something. Have to tell Nikhil about Amit.* Stuck in dilemma, talking to himself Vivek held the steering. Sheena sat beside him. Now their vehicles were moving ahead to the address given by Charan.

Steering by one hand, his other hand was holding the forehead, Vivek was skeptical about Amit. He couldn't take a stand.

"What happened?" Sheena asked. Watching Vivek silent for so long she had understood his confusion. "Seem upset?"

"I do not know! It looks like something went by from in front of my eyes and there is this Amit's ..." "Amit, what about him?" She immediately asked.

Amit was peddling his brain wires. Vivek did not want this thing out yet, but now he was thinking of telling Sheena about Amit. There was something else which was striking his mind like the hammer. Just then from the right side, Nikhil's vehicle came near to his vehicle and his eye fell on Nikhil. Nikhil was mashing his eyes corner. Watching Nikhil doing this, God knows what had happened to Vivek. He saw the traffic back from the mirror and immediately turned the car, turning the steering on the road between.

"Hey!!!" Inadvertent Sheena blew from her seat and got stuck at the side of the door. "What are you doing?"

"We have been fooled, Sheena!" Vivek said. He was taking the way back.

Chapter Twelve

An honest mistake

* * *

Time : evening 5:45 pm.

"Reverse! Reverse Nayak! Reverse!" Seeing this activity of Vivek's, Nikhil also shouted at Amit. Amit had already turned the steering around to turn the car.

Within five minutes, their vehicles reached back the same complex. Quickly the vehicles stopped instantly out of the complex. Vivek opened the door and went out like a storm.

"Charan is Dr. David." Vivek said, reaching out to the stairs. "What are you saying?" Said Nikhil immediately. So far, Vivek had climbed upstairs by jumping. All the other three were also forced to go after him.

"Doctor David is a forty-five years old and he is a thirty years old man." Sheena said. "And he is not even a 'kandil.'" Sheena's intention was about Doctor David's spectacles.

"No offense." said Sheena looking to Nikhil.

"None was taken." He replied.

"He was writing with his left hand if you guys didn't notice and doctor David is holding the tube in the same hand." Moving towards the lift, Nikhil took out his mobile and saw that image, entering the lift. The image confirmed the correctness of Vivek's point.

"Being a lefty is not an unusual thing?" Nikhil said.

Vivek said stating another point. "That's right. But I remembered during the conversation with us, he mashed his eyes just like you just..." "...did in the vehicle." Nikhil snatched the words from Vivek's mouth.

"Everything else may be wrong, but the Jesus' locket around his neck, which can not be mistaken, a Christian man wears. I saw a glimpse of that while returning, slipped out of focus."

The last one removed suspicions inside all. All questions disappeared from their faces. The door of the lift opened and they moved on but had to stop. Because of the crowd, it was unable to see anything ahead.

"Take him to the hospital!"

"Call an ambulance!"

"He is still breathing!"

These noises sounded from the crowd. Vivek stopped Sheena by fears of anything uncertain. They moved ahead, repelling people. Charan was down in front of them. There was a hole in the chest, which was bleeding. Nikhil and Vivek immediately came to him and Vivek picked him up with his hands. Amit immediately drew his gun and promptly took a tour of the whole place. He quickly went down to the stairs tearing around the crowd. After reaching out, he rotated his eyes in every direction but unfortunately, he did not see any suspected person. He began to return with disappointed on his face.

Meanwhile Nikhil and Vivek, holding doctor had

entered the lift and were heading down.

"I have called the emergency. They will be here soon." Said Nikhil hanging up the call. Vivek was looking upset. "What happened?" Nikhil asked.

"I'm unable to read his mind." Said in a worried tone. It was not the best time for this but it was very important. Vivek had to read his mind.

"Keep trying." Nikhil asserted.

"I am, but it's not happening." Said Vivek keeping that same tone.

Shit! Shit! I have to do this. I have to do this. "Vivek!" Nikhil's voice broke his thoughts.

Vivek saw Nikhil, his eyes were looking toward where the doctor was held. Vivek slowly looked down. Doctor's pulse had stopped, he had turned into a dead man now. Just then the door opened. Vivek came out with a heavy heart, stepping his legs slowly on the floor. One more down and they couldn't do anything.

"I think it's the only drawback of your power my son." Vivek's father's voice began to reverberate in his ears. That moment when Nikhil and Amit started their necessary work Vivek reached to his thought land.

"What are we gonna do about this Papa?" Thirteen-year-old Vivek asked his father. They were still in the same place, same time. The roof of the home at 10 0' clock in the morning.

Despondent Devesh replied. "We are trying this for like a year. Maybe.. Maybe we can't do anything about it."

Father of Vivek, just like any normal dad in appearance, 5'6" tall, a little protruding tummy, impressive looking mustache below the nose, thick hair and a healthy body. Smarter than usual ones as what Vivek thought. A man who always found a solution to every problem, Vivek didn't expect this type of an answer from him. It disappointed him. His hanging mouth explained everything to Devesh.

He came near him and said giving him hope. "It's a rule of nature. When it gives something to someone, also sets a limit and this is yours that may be sometimes....in under pressure, you will not be able to read mind."

"Vivek! Vivek!!" Hearing his name from Nikhil's mouth, Lost Vivek returned in reality. That same thing had happened in Sardar boy's case. He saw the corpse of the doctor, laid in stretcher had been kept in an ambulance.

Chapter Thirteen

Love to the destination

* * *

Almost 4 months ago from Today. Sep-tember 2015.

"Okkk then, I'll leave now." Said Vivek, was on his blue Pulsar bike. Sheena was getting off from the bike. They were standing in front of Sheena's apartment's main gate.

"Okay." She said but didn't go from there.

They were watching each other. For next three moments, it looked like their lips were trying to stop something very badly. Upper and lower lips were pressed against each other. One more moment passed, the two first unchained their suppressed laugh together, sounded like a bike is trying to get started.

"Hahahahahahahahahaha." Ultimately they both laughed out loud. The watchman, who was minding his own business till now, began to stare at them.

"I told you she was gonna slap him, but you didn't believe me." Vivek said while laughing.

"It was hilarious. I had never seen a live scene like this. Best day of my life." She kept laughing too. Her hands went towards her tummy. "But..." She took a pause. "How did you know?" and she dropped the bomb.

"Talent." Vivek delivered an obvious answer, cleverly hiding the fact.

"Kuchh bhi na.." She said and turned toward the main gate.

"Sheena!!" She just took three steps ahead when Vivek called her name.

She, without losing a second, turned back and asked. "What??"

"Amm..I.." Vivek hesitated. "Um..." He was trying to say something but words were not taking his side. "Nothing...you go. I'll tell you later." At last, he had to give up. He started his bike and left. Sheena was watching him go. She smiled and went back to the apartment.

She reached to her flat's main door. She opened the lock of the door and before she could enter inside, a kid came to her and said. "This is for you."

Sheena saw that the boy was having a box wrapped. "Who gave you this?"

"A boy came when you weren't here, gave me this and told that you will understand once you open it." She got confused, took that gift box from the kid and thanked him.

She entered inside her flat, staring at the box as she was thinking about the man who gave it. She unwrapped the box and opened it. It was a footwear box with a pair of high heels under it.

"Wow." Delight appeared all over her face. There was a small greeting card below heels. She restrained her excitement over curiosity and placed the box on the table carefully, opened the greeting card and began reading.

"A gift in advance for the birthday girl as an advance wish. They do not look as beautiful as you but I'm sure they will, once you wear them. I hope you'll like it.

You're the most beautiful girl I've ever seen. Always be happy and thanks to born in this world and for making me your friend. HAPPY BIRTHDAY, Sheena.

Your new and divine friend."

She finished reading the card. She had a big smile on her face, which was hard to stop. She put the card on the table. Her thumbs started pressing on the mobile screen. Some touches later, she put the mobile on her ears.

"How did you know about birthday and heels?" She asked. She was thinking about those heels from past many days. Due to the expensive price, she couldn't buy.

"That's not the question. The question is... did you like the gift?" It was Vivek's voice from the other side of the phone.

"Very much." She said. Vivek can sense her happiness even in the phone. "But how did..." She again tried to ask that question.

"ZizZZziz..." Vivek avoided again by producing that voice. "Aam khao, guthliyaan kyun gin rahi ho?" He made her speechless.

She chuckled. "Okay. See you tomorrow." She said and hung up her cell.

One month had passed since they met. Vivek was now friends with Sheena. They were having a great time together. The two just came from a theater of Korba, after enjoying a nice love story movie. It was coincident that they both were living here in Korba and went to Bilaspur that day for some import-ant work and met to each other.

The next morning of their first meeting, Vivek offered her a lift which she accepted. The conversation started between them on the way. This way they came to know about each other. Vivek was go-ing very smoothly. He was very careful about his feelings to not open up. Sheena also seemed to enjoy his company and talks. He was making her laugh.

Sheena was staying in her friend's room. After dropping her there, he asked her out. She accepted to thank him. They went for a movie and this is how their friendship began.

Today, Vivek couldn't sleep. He wanted to asleep but his eyes were not agreeing. Anyhow he convinced them to close. But devils started to show him Sheena's image repeatedly. This devilment was going on from the past one month and was increasing night by night. That night he kept awake and he took a decision.

"I'm gonna tell her today about my feelings." He told his decision to himself, standing in front of the mirror. "But how…?" He put a finger on his chin and started thinking. After hard work of half an hour, sitting on the commode, he reached a point when he found out a way to tell her.

"Oh what the hell, how tough it could be? I am just gonna tell her. Will see after that." And finalized that.

Time- 7.00 pm in the evening.

"Number fourth, down to left is doctor Bheem Rao Ambedkar. The sixth one, right to forward is Akshay Kumar. Number seven is Amrapali, top to bottom. Number eleven should be Vilasrao Deshmukh bottom to left. Twelve, down to right is definitely Shahrukh Khan my favourite and the fifteen, left to the top is...move your finger a little bit...ahaa!! Rajat Sharma." Vivek extracted Sheena's attention by finishing crosswords in seconds. She was trying to fill that up from last half an hour.

"So easy." He said. Sheena was looking at him angrily. "What? What happened??" He asked.

"Do you know for how long I had been waiting for you?" She scolded him.

"Yeah! I know. I was watching you from there." He pointed to the direction where a copied and smaller structure of Taj Mahal was situated.

"But why from the...." Suddenly she paused and patted her forehead lightly. "Sorry, sorry, sorry!! I forgot you told me to meet there. Sorry!"

"Doesn't matter. It's your birthday. And even if it's not, you're allowed." He said taking the newspaper from her. "It's good to see that in the mobile age you still solve crosswords." He praised her.

"And it's good to know that I have a very smart friend who can solve this in seconds." She praised him back.

It was a big beautiful park named 'Silver Jubilee'. Apart from Taj mahal, they had the big area of gardens and a large pond with boating available. The park was situated about ten to twelve kilometer away from the main city.

"So, you wanted to say something to me?" She brought up the matter that Vivek had told her about over the phone.

"Yaa!! Actually...ahammm." He first hesitated and cleared his throat.

*What the f*ck. Why am I being so nervous?*

"Say." She interrupted.

"Umm.. Let's go there then we will talk." The only words came from his mouth out of courage.

Damn...I am a big fattu. There was an inner conflict going between his mind and heart. The heart was forcing him to pop out the matter while the mind was holding him not to say anything.

"It's fifteen minutes now, I am waiting to hear something more except ummm, aaa, ahammm. Are you going to say something or did you just called me for time-pass." She said impatiently.

God! Here I am having difficulty in telling her my heart out and her looks are making it all the more difficult. Why did she wear that white salwar suit with her curly hairstyle? And that earrings, damn to those.

"Oh shit!!" Sheena shouted. Her voice broke his thoughts. She was looking at her mobile.

"What happened?" He asked.

"I have to go." She said. "My friends are throwing a birthday party for me. And I can't be late. They'll kill me. We'll talk some other time." She added.

Vivek now realized. "Tomorrow then?" He said.

"No! I am going to Bilaspur, will return after two days."

"Okay then let me talk till we reach the parking." He said when he saw her going forward.

"Okay."

Here starts a rapid-fire round between them where Vivek was asking and Sheena was answering.

"Where is the party?"

"Grill-In, T.P. Nagar."

"Who else is gonna there?"

"My all friends I have told you about."

"Is going Bilaspur tomorrow necessary?"

"Yes. Because my boss says."

"I think I love you."

"Yaa. I love you too."

Time stopped at that moment. Their feet stopped walking. They both were not looking to each other right now. Vivek's mouth opened where Sheena covered her lips with her hand. They slowly turned towards each other. They could hear the wind blowing as music. They kept gazing at each other for seconds. Then later, Sheena moved a little and resumed her speed. Vivek kept watching her go away. She reached her scooty and went from there.

Time- 9.00 pm at night.

He got late. Party had started. He was not invited but he reached. He didn't even go there, where Sheena's friends were celebrating her birthday. He was just looking at her, sitting alone on a chair from a short distance, pretending to eat. Sheena noticed him but couldn't do anything. Vivek was seeing her, realizing that she was not there at the moment, she was thinking about something. There was something bothering her.

Her friends went to their ways after party finished. Vivek was following her. After some turns, he realized where Sheena was going. It was Vivek's home. She stopped her scooty in front of his home's main gate. Vivek opened the lock and they both parked their vehicles. He opened the main door and the two entered in. Vivek threw keys on a sofa. They were both silents till now.

"Look, I want to say that ummmm....." Before he

could complete his sentence he felt her lips against his lips. His heartbeat rose. First, his upper lip was between her two lips then his lower lip. She did it for two minutes, one hand was caressing his hair while another one was on his back, then Vivek took his hands to her waist and pressed her against himself. It was his time to execute. Their bodies didn't have any space for air to pass in between.

Vivek grabbed her thighs lifted her up and came to his bedroom, near the bed, without interrupting the kiss. They both dropped their bodies on the bed. Even they didn't have any idea when their clothes left their bodies. Vivek's silent room was spreading some pleasant screams tonight.

It was 2 O' clock at night. Both were very tired. Vivek was in deep sleep for sure as he still had a smile on his face. Sheena was sleeping too. Her eyes were closed, next moment she opened her eyes. Vivek was next to her, facing his face opposite towards her face. She got up, went towards the bathroom but didn't go there. She was taking her steps very silently.

She, taking a look at Vivek, confirming his sleep stopped at the book arrangement near the television. She started to prune them very quietly and carefully. It looked like she was finding something. Finally, after looking at six books, she stopped at seventh one which was a usual size copy.

She started turning its pages. Before rolling over another, she looked at the sketches carefully. She reached the last drawing. It was a sketch of her heels, gifted by Vivek yesterday.

She closed the copy, put it back where it was and arranged all books as it originally was. Without making any sound she returned to the bed and laid. Took her mobile and sent a message to a contact num-ber.

The message was...'It's confirmed, he was not telling a lie that night. Vivek can read minds. I'll wait for your next instruction.'

Chapter fourteen

Hide and Seek

* * *

Time: evening 6:15 pm today.

People began gathering near the complex. The complex already had enough rush. After a while, people from the other complex also began to come. Nikhil cleared the main passage and stairs. People were sent out and banned from coming and going. They were now standing on the sides and were compelled to find their own speculation.

Doctor David had taken most measures to keep himself a secret. With the name, he had also changed his religion and transformed his age. Yet, so much caution couldn't prevent his death. Raghav not only killed him but also he deplumed fake appearance on his face.

At the time of the accident, there were no witnesses. Nobody on that complex had seen any person looking like Raghav. Before the arrival of the team, they had to investigate from their side and the same result came out here nothing. Doctor David's body outside his studio, was in front of the shop which was not rented yet, so there was no one to watch.

"We had gone for about five minutes. We then returned and he was killed. That means we made a little mistake which gave Raghav to do his job. While returning back from the studio, I saw a glimpse of that locket on his neck, wish I would have noticed at that time. But... but my focus was so much on someone else." Vivek uttered by showing his disappointment. Sheena standing in front of him was watching him. She was sensing his feelings very well.

"What's the use of such power if it cannot save the life of an innocent," he said.

"Look! I do not want to hurt you. But I still suggest you should separate yourself from all this. It is not for you or me." Sheena's hands on the cheeks of Vivek while reminding feel of her softness were trying to reduce his frustration and growing anger.

"No Sheena! Now I will not rest until Raghav is caught." The anger that Sheena did not want to come out had already made their way into the Vivek's mind. Sheena said nothing further. "It's my fault I hid one thing from you and Nikhil but now I'm gonna..."

".. Oh no!" Sheena interrupted in between and said. Her eyes were shocked suddenly by looking elsewhere.

"What happened?"

"Raghav has fair skin in appearance?" Sheena asked.

"Yes."

"Beard face, goggles on eyes, black thick hair coming down to the neck and black clothes?" Vivek had already told the phiz of Raghav to Sheena.

Listening to the face description of Raghav in such a way, Vivek got surprised. "You...How do you know?" He asked.

"I am looking at a man just like that in front. He is watching everything from the other side of the crowd. Apart from his phiz, I'm having doubts because he is the only one there whose expressions are different from the whole crowd, like a dead face. He is not trying to lift up his head to watch. He is not looking interested in talking to anyone."

Vivek's eyebrows and eyes raveled. "Are you sure?" Vivek stopped his thrilled heart as he wanted to look back so badly but without turning back he spoke to Sheena.

Sheena replied. "Wait, I'll show you." Sheena took out his mobile and immediately took a photo, showed Vivek.

"That's him." Vivek confirmed. "Then tell them both immediately," Sheena suggested.

"No!"

"Why?"

"We do not have time." Vivek gave a valid point but there was another reason. He didn't want to let know Amit about him.

"Now what?"

"Do whatever I say."

Vivek explained Sheena the plan. They were standing outside the complex. Out there was a huge crowd muttering to each other, constrained by their habit and curiosity. The news channels created a separate distance and were reporting news. Vivek and Sheena were a part of the crowd of right to left. Sheena had seen Raghav at the left of the crowd, where there was a way to go to the underground parking. Seeing Raghav, it seemed like his eyes were searching for someone.

Vivek was explaining something to Sheena. Sheena shook her head and took out his cell phone, typed a cell number. A few seconds later, Vivek's mobile rang, he took out his mobile. Sheena called him. Vivek pressed the call receiving option then took out his Bluetooth headset from jacket's side-pocket and put it to ears.

"Easy." Sheena said to Vivek.

Now Vivek turned slowly and began to retreat. Sheena was the navigator for him right now and was giving him direction. Vivek was taking steps according to her.

"Approximately thirty people between you and him. All are looking to front or at each-other, but Raghav seems to be looking for somebody therefore whatever happens do not look in that direction."

"Got it." Vivek said in sotto voce.

Sheena said after Vivek crossed the four men. "To your right next, a fat man is going to come, take two steps back and then keep going in the right direction." Vivek did so.

"Wait!!" After alerting Sheena, Vivek immediately stopped there. "Take two steps back and cover yourself behind that fat boy."

Sheena was keeping an eye on Raghav's movements carefully. Therefore there was no room for questions of not complying with her instructions. Vivek immediately took the guise of course. Raghav's eyes were drifting towards him but because he was hidden behind thick body Vivek slipped from him. "Raghav's presence here is not making any sense." Sheena said.

"It will, once I catch him." Vivek replied.

Raghav's moving eyes reached Sheena. Sheena immediately moved her eyes from Vivek and began to look to the other way. Raghav had not seen Sheena, this goes in her favor.

Vivek, still standing behind the fat man was waiting for her guidelines. Raghav was still looking towards that direction. Suddenly the fat man stepped behind from his place. Vivek was unaware but Sheena had seen this.

"Take a step back, quickly. He will see you." She said immediately.

Vivek without losing a single moment took steps backward. Raghav, at the same time, rotate the eye passing through that side. So far, Vivek was hide again behind the fat man. Raghav from this side now seemed carefree. He now began to see in the opposite direction from their direction.

Sheena again stuck her eyes on Raghav. "Oh no!" Said Sheena.

"What happened?" Vivek said instantly.

"He's probably going back."

"I will..."

"Make no mistake. There are many people here and he had the gun in his hand. He is going back slowly. We can still catch him from behind." Sheena stopped him by making realize the big mistake in rushing. "We will hold him from the shortcuts... now you just have to walk sideways. There are only ten people between. A short and skinny boy is right behind you. Start walking from there then approximately you'll reach to Raghav."

Vivek now increased the speed of his steps. Raghav's back appeared after crossing the eighth men. Now it was just a few moments to catch him. Raghav hadn't the slightest realization that Vivek, behind him was ready to hunt like a hunter.

At the same time, Nikhil and Amit came down. Raghav's eyes fell on Nikhil. Nikhil was looking at Sheena. Raghav, through Nikhil, saw Sheena. Then he followed her eyes. Sheena was looking at Vivek who was behind Raghav. Turning back, Raghav's body started shuddering at the same time as he strongly guessed that Vivek was behind him.

The game of sight, Nikhil's unawareness of the activity of Vivek and Sheena's made a lapse.

Raghav turned but found that Vivek was not behind him. Raghav turned back to Nikhil and Sheena to confirm her involvement with him but fortunately, Sheena also saw this sudden change of circumstances. Before Nikhil could come close to Sheena, she stepped back into crowd.

Sheena searched for Vivek but he had disappeared. Confused Sheena did the same for Raghav but he had also disappeared.

Chapter fifteen

Little chit-chat

* * *

Time: Evening 6.30pm.

Where the hell is he? Sheena thought, her eyes were searching Vivek.

"Hello! Hello!!" Sheena tried to communicate with him. *He didn't hang up yet then why isn't he answering?* She looked and confirmed his connection on the phone.

"What happened? Who are you looking for and where is Vivek?" Nikhil approached to Sheena cutting the crowd. Amit was behind him.

Sheena told them the whole plan.

"What?? Raghav was here and you guys didn't tell us?" Nikhil unintentionally yelled at her. His voice rose at the moment.

"I told you. We had no other option." Sheena said softening Nikhil. Amit's hand already grabbed his gun and started to look around. He didn't find Vivek or Raghav. Pushing people, Amit and Nikhil exceeded scrum.

Two police officers of Champa also joined Nikhil. He told them to stay with him.

"Shsssshhs!!" Sheena by producing noise gestured them to be quiet. "It's Vivek. Voice is low but audible enough." Sheena said.

She heard Vivek's voice over the phone. They all shut their mouth. Sheena put the phone on speaker.

"I am in the parking after Raghav." They heard Vivek's whispering voice. All began to enter the parking. They had their guns out in their hands, grabbed firmly.

"Stop!!" Nikhil suddenly said to Amit, Sheena and the two officers behind him. "I am hearing voices.... oh No!! They are fighting. Let's go." Nikhil instantly ordered and he and other officers started scramming. "Perhaps Raghav somehow found out about Vivek following him." He informed all running.

They were about to reach inside enough when a car swiftly passed from the side. It was at quite a speed. But somehow they saw a glimpse of Vivek seating on the back seat, at Raghav's gunpoint next to him. Someone else was driving the car.

"After all, what happened?" Nikhil asked with a question mark on his face. Sheena and Amit's face expressions were asking the same question.

The answer came from Sheena's phone. "You tried a smart move but I'm smarter than you Vivek." A very rough voice mentioning Vivek was surely Raghav's. "Smart because you didn't let me know that you were after me and smarter because I found out at the last moment, attacked at you and made you my hostage."

Vivek had another smart move which Raghav didn't know about. Before following Raghav to the parking, he put his Bluetooth headset in the pocket and did not hang up the call. And then he kept his mobile in his front shirt pocket. Raghav was taking Vivek somewhere, unaware about this. The car had disappeared from the view. But now through Sheena's phone, they were able to chase Raghav.

"Are you going to admit me in B.D.M. Dharam hospital?" Vivek, saying this, gave them a hint.

Nikhil got ready immediately and instructed. "We got the direction. Let's go." They knew the location as, while entering Champa they saw the hospital.

The two officers already started their vehicle. "You both follow him from an alternate path. Police gypsey could alert him. I'll keep informing you." Nikhil instructed them.

Amit and Nikhil reached their vehicle. Nikhil said to Sheena who was behind them. "You stay here, we will rescue him." They both took her mobile and sat on their seats, Amit on driving seat and Nikhil next to him. As they started their vehicle the second moment Sheena climbed behind into the vehicle.

"I'm not gonna wait here." She told them in an immovable tone. They understood what Vivek told them about her, was very true. Without losing any second they moved and started following the car. Driving at high speed, Amit soon came near the car. Now he maintained an average distance and stayed behind an-other SUV vehicle so that Raghav couldn't notice them.

Here Vivek, seated next to Raghav, was trying to let everything out from his mouth. "So you had a friend too?" Said Vivek about the guy who was driving. He was dark skin colored boy around twenty-five year old by looks with little beard face and messy hairs.

"Just approached him after entering Champa.

'THEY' provided me." Raghav said.

Vivek smiled as he succeeded in his first attempt and asked further. "They?? Organization or team of 2-3 people?"

"You don't need to know." He replied.

"Very good. He is trying to make him confess." Nikhil said happily where Sheena and Amit's face were changing their countenance.

There were shops on either side of the main road and alternate paths linked. They had openings after every ten to fifteen shops which were connecting the main roads to internal ones. The other police officers were chasing the car from the right side of the internal path.

"You're going to get caught." Vivek tried to manipulate him.

They crossed the hospital. Raghav saw him for a moment and then said sitting comfortably. He had his gun carefully on his hand so that Vivek couldn't snatch it.

"No! They're not. Want to see how?" Raghav said. "Let me show you."

There was a red signal ahead. All vehicles stopped. Raghav instructed the guy to take car next to a bus. He did it. Raghav signaled Vivek to get down from the car.

"Your any clever movement can be injurious to your and the health of people around here." Raghav said accompanying him.

Raghav made Vivek helpless. At least Raghav was considering that. They both got on the bus. The signal turned green from red. The vehicle started to move forward. The bus went straight. On the other hand, that boy was captured by Nikhil and Amit, before he could take any turn as they were behind him hidden in vehicle crowd. They got him in the vehicle. The biggest advantage of Vivek's smart move.

There were two types of the row into the bus. One with three seaters and another one with two seaters. Due to less crowd, Raghav managed to sit in three seater with Vivek leaving a seat in the middle. He put his bag in the middle seat.

Sheena's company proved useful for Nikhil and Amit. After capturing the boy Sheena handled driving seat where the two started interrogating him.

Amit put his gun on boy's forehead.

Nikhil said angrily."Dekh be !! I don't have time to know your name. Just tell me who contacted you to join Raghav?"

Seeing police in front, his voice stuck in his throat. "I..I.. don't know." He answered. Amit pressed his gun more against his forehead. "Really... I can only tell that whoever is behind this is not alone. And if I am not wrong then a policeman is involved."

"What nonsense?" Nikhil shocked and yelled.

"Yes! And I heard from him about someone named 'One-Four-Three', perhaps it was a codeword. I don't know more than this. Leave me, please leave me." He started crying.

Amit and Nikhil's experience told them that the boy is no longer useful. Amit hit his head with the gun and made him swoon. They got a big, shocking and strange information. Now they were waiting for Vivek to dig out some more.

"Where are you going?" Vivek tried one more time.

Raghav got up from his seat and said. "Don't come

into view again. I am not paid for killing you." He knew that Vivek is not going to do anything due to the gun on his belt and people around him. There was another signal ahead. Vivek was a ticket for him to escape from police and his work has done. He stepped ahead.

Stepping forward, Raghav suddenly froze there. "Don't get conscious about me but you're gonna go to hell for sure." He said smiling deviously. Extracting his gun out and pointing to Vivek, said Raghav. "Why don't you come with me." Raghav sensed the danger and suddenly changed his mind.

Seeing gun on Raghav's hand, everybody on the bus freaked out and started screaming. Raghav showed them a look of his gun. They all became silent like good kids as they weren't ready to see God yet.

"Oh no!" Said Nikhil frightfully. "We have to rescue Vivek. Now." Nikhil said looking in front.

There was another red signal about to come. They both prepared themselves. Nikhil called another officers to be ready.

Here Raghav was standing near the door putting Vivek on aim in front of him as the shield.

They arrived at the signal. All vehicles stopped. Nikhil and Amit quickly came out from the vehicle. Raghav, pushing Vivek, also came out from the bus. The passengers took a deep breath and relaxed. Raghav hit very hard with his gun on Vivek's head. Vivek lost his balance for a while. Seeing this, Nikhil immediately ran towards Raghav. Amit also followed him.

Meanwhile Raghav had arrogated another car from a man, showing him his gun. Raghav started the vehicle. Both were one meter apart from the car. Nikhil heard the start sound and increased his speed further.

Till now, Raghav had moved a little. Nikhil jumped running and grabbed the car's left side roof rack strongly. Raghav entered in the middle of traffic knocking off the other vehicles coming from green signal direction and Nikhil went along with him.

This entire event just took fifteen seconds. Vivek maintained himself and ran behind the car. He was about to go between the running traffic when two hands grabbed him from behind and pulled towards the back-side. It was Amit. Right at that moment, just from there, a black colored car passed. Amit rescued Vivek from committing suicide.

"Leave me. Nikhil is in danger." Clutched by Amit, Vivek fluttered.

"Calm down. You were about to end your life." Loosening Vivek, Amit said yelling. He took him to an empty area there.

"Yes! I should calm down." Vivek had Amit's gun in his hand pointed on Amit. "Because you're the one who is going to catch Raghav and save Nikhil." He added.

Sheena was coming from behind Amit, surprised by Vivek's act, asked him. "What the hell are you doing??"

Amit got a chance and he didn't miss it, he instantly caught her. Grabbed her with his left hand and put his right hand to her head. "Give me the gun otherwise I'll break her neck."

Both the officers, Unenlightened from this critical situation, had been crossed traffic to ensure Raghav when signal turned green.

Chapter Sixteen

Messing with crocodile

* * *

Time : evening 6:50 pm.

Vivek raised an audacious step but Amit turned the events, he left no choice for Vivek. He gestured Vivek to bounce the gun. Helpless Vivek had to do that. Amit caught the gun and pushed Sheena towards Vivek.

"Get a side." Said Amit, waved them by gun to come together. "No smart moves." He warned.

Vivek's face was evidence of having taken his decision. Now there was only one question on his face that why Amit is doing this all. Amit was also aware of these questions.

"I know what are you thinking?" "Right-wrong is in front of me. I do not need to think about anything else." Vivek's rage was boiling inside but regardless of Sheena's life had forced him to remain cool.

"When Sir approached me with this case without telling me anything, I did not have any issues. Then I met you and you surprised me by your behavior. I did not know what to do. Nikhil and I did not share any good bond. I had my transfer in Korba only four months ago. He was always listening to you. Whereas, I knew the commissioner well and trusted him. So I had no choice other than to talk to him.

"I did not understand?" Vivek seems confused.

"I mean, you were the first suspect for me. You knew the murderer, knew the targets and even the next ones. Then gave a reason which was hard to believe, I had to do something, therefore I kept reporting to the commissioner, until.."

"Until...?"

"Until I didn't trust you myself. I've seen you put your life at stake, so I trust you now."

"And why should I trust you?"

Amit laid his shotgun in his hand and presented in front of him, said. "Because I'm also ready to risk my life. You keep it and decide. I leave my life at your mercy. You can read my mind if you want to."

Vivek's eyes were assaying Amit. He was looking the truth and honesty in Amit's eyes.

"Let's find Nikhil." Vivek closed his fist which had a gun and said.

Sheena did not agree with his decision. She said protesting. "What are you doing Vivek?" Hearing their words now Sheena also understood Amit's hidden things. Doubts for Amit just had occurred in her mind which hadn't removed, unlike Vivek.

"Let's go, Sheena! By doubting Amit we have already put Nikhil in danger. Let's contact him." Vivek said, holding her hand going towards the vehicle. Sheena had parked it near. Amit also turned to the vehicle.

Going toward the vehicle, Sheena pulled out her hidden question. "Are you sure you did the right thing by trusting on Amit?" She asked whispering.

Vivek said. "There are few peoples who risk their life to prove the truth! I did not see an even little bit of fear in his eyes when he left his gun in front of me." Vivek had left Sheena unanswered.

****

Four days ago from today. January 2016. Maharashtra.

Sheena was standing outside a hotel. For fifteen minutes she had been standing there waiting for someone. A black colored car came in front of her. She sat in the car and moved. After coming off from the city limits, the car entered in a very sparsely populated area surrounded by trees. The number of trees grew. Now the terrain was becoming wild and dense. Only one house was visible there. The car stopped and the owner of a thinner body came out. Face's skin color was fair and light beard had grown.

Sheena came out from the car and said, addressing the boy. "Thanks, Asif."

Asif came forward, raising the hand and pointed. "This way."

In front, there was a small house. Sheena and Asif walked inside. Entering inside, there was a large room. On the opposite side of the door, few things were laid on a table. A large round chair next to the table and the other side there were two more chairs. Showing his back, a man in black colored coat and pant, standing near round chair was looking outside of the window.

Sheena behind Asif came in and stood near the two chairs. Her high heel's 'tuck -tuck' has cleared stillness from the entire room. At that time, she was looking at an athleticism-sized man.

The man said in a thundering voice. "Asif! You can go!" Asif immediately went out from the hall.

"Sit down."

Sheena sat. Turning back, Sheena looked at Asif. She said turning back her head after he stepping out. "Things are exactly going like what you had said. Because of your teaching techniques, I'm able to divert my attention to other things whereby nothing came on my mind even by mistake and Vivek could not read anything from my mind. He didn't know that I know about his powers."

The man turned back to Sheena and said. "Hmm!! Now the another important thing," this man was Shivraam Dharmatma.

Chapter seventeen

Virus

* * *

Time : Night 7:10 pm today.

Raghav reached to a Scrapyard, running car recklessly. Nikhil was still holding firmly to the roof rack. Raghav instead of coming from the main street was entered by colonies and local streets. Everyone, opening their mouths, enjoyed this bravery act of Nikhil. A few people were dialing the phone but they didn't have anything to tell but details of the view and vehicle number. People didn't even know that they are calling the police to help a policeman. The officers who were after him had already gotten rid off.

Raghav was driving the car in a direct manner yet. Once reached the scrap yard, he stopped his car with a loud stroke. Nikhil's hand ultimately abandoned and he landed on the ground after turning about two-three times. After stopping, he handled himself, dusted his clothes and sat on his knee. He was about to stand when a barrel struck on his forehead. He looked up, Raghav was in front who had the gun in his hand. He had been standing in front of him like the 'Yamraaj', God of death. Raghav's finger slowly began to push back thetrigger. Scrapyard was deserted and his friends, right now, were also far away to save him.

To that moment Nikhil was ready to say goodbye to the world, but the next moment Raghav removed his finger from the trigger and took barrel from the forehead of Nikhil. “Felt like you’re gonna kill me for real.” Nikhil said standing.

“Felt like you’re gonna catch me for real.” Raghav said keeping shotgun back. “What was the need to pursue me so hard?” He asked.

“If I had not done it, then Amit or Vivek would have done it which would ruin the plan.” Nikhil extracted almond this time from another pocket and began to eat. His voice of eating and tone of talking again started a rhythm.

“Once Raghav grabs a gun in hand, no one can stop him from finishing his work.”

Nikhil offered him almonds and said. “Idiot!! Even Big ‘Turram khans’ hanged to death because of the overconfidence. This time I saw obsession inside Vivek to catch you.”

Raghav stared at Nikhil on his ‘word-pinch’. Nikhil kept his almond back.

Raghav’s fished a cigarette from his pocket and said, opening. “If lamp light flounces, it doesn’t mean it can burn the house. This means only,” Raghav brought pack close to the mouth, and he pulled out a cigarette. “He’s going to be put out.” Cigarette between his lips suppressed the voice.

“Vivek was not ‘switching off the lamp’ this time, he was going to prove a bright spark which can fire the entire haystack only by a flick.” Nikhil ate almond by catching on his mouth in a stylish way and said. "Vivek wanted you to catch him in the parking so that you tell him everything by yourself. He was connected with us through the phone the entire time. I had to interrogate that boy but fortunately, he didn't know much but the codeword you named me and my partner." He added.

"One four three?" Raghav chuckles. "I wonder what would happen when he came to know about your second partner."

Nikhil stopped for a second and said to him in a bossy style. "You just do what you're paid for. I'm sick of saving you. At Korba, I had to inform you through the message that Amit and Vivek were behind you, at the Magneto mall and now when I saw you getting trapped in Vivek's game, I had to risk my life. Don't ever underestimate him. If you give his intelligence a chance, he'll not leave you worth doing."

He alerted Raghav and praised Vivek further. "He thinks that he have only three super skills but I know he has four, brilliant mind capable of planning in critical situations is the last one."

"Why don't you let me kill him?"

"No, you would not kill him. Not yet." Given serious look to Raghav, Nikhil admonished him.

Raghav began to go back, then suddenly stopped and said, without looking at his face. "Whose side are you on, me or him?"

"I'm on my side. I'll kill him myself. You just do what you are told to do." Said Nikhil.

Raghav had the car door opened. He said clarifying himself. "I thought doctor David was not dead, so I went there to confirm."

"I know. Work on the next step of the plan. You know where to go for your next target." Nikhil came near Raghav's car, said.

"And Vivek's power, what about that?"

"Just like I didn't let him touch me yet, I'm not gonna let him do the same in future". So saying, Nikhil gestured him to move. Raghav went.

After he left, Nikhil called Amit and gave him, his location details and sat there.

Vivek and Amit oblivious to all this, arrived there in like fifteen minutes driving their vehicle fast. They found Nikhil sitting on the bonnet of a scrap car, forlorn. His face was scratched; Shirt and jeans were ripped slightly.

Stopping the SUV, Vivek came to Nikhil running quickly and asked. "Are you okay?"

Everyone, unaware of Nikhil, being a wolf in lamb's clothing, were happy to see Nikhil safe.

Nikhil also stood from his place."Fine. But I would not surely be if he had not rushed to escape." Nikhil replied very smartly.

"We cannot do anything now? We, on our hands, have not a clue nor Raghav." Said Nikhil. There was no any lack his acting. "Now the last member is left only and we don't know where to find him." Amit joined the chorus with the same sense of Nikhil.

"Just a codeword name one four three. What does that indicate anyway, I love you, I hate you?" Vivek dazed and started pondering about it.

"The boy didn't know? And the man who could open the mystery slipped from our hand." Nikhil said, demoralizing them.

Vivek said lighting the lamp of hope among their disappointments. "I have a little clue. It would probably work." It was all he said, all eyes turned towards him.

"When I had a fight with Raghav, He came in contact with me for a while, I saw something which was going on in his mind." Vivek said further.

Listening to Vivek, Nikhil's expressions start changing. But before anyone could read his face changes he got back to normal and said. "What did you see?"

Vivek in response went to the police vehicle and brought a page from inside and he again began to make something. The three watched him for a while. In front of Vivek, they all became like the audience who had come to watch a magic and were not able to find magician's exploit until the end.

Vivek holds on and all eyes stuck on the page. "Swachh Bharat Abhiyan?" Sheena said.

There was a strip on the page on which it was written. As well as some sort of chairs were made. Amit understood the meaning of it. He took the copy and told. "Swachh Bharat Abhiyan program will be in five Districts in the state today. Perhaps the next member is in one of these towns."

Nikhil tried to confuse them. "Now, how will we identify that one district among these districts so soon?"

They all started cogitating.

"No use of this," after a while, when no one got-any idea, Vivek kicked a stone aloud lying on the floor with rage. "..picture."

Stone hit on a poster. The poster was on a pillar, on the wall outside the limits of the Scrapyard. His eyes were on the poster. Suddenly, he was beginning to move, gazing at the poster. Perhaps some idea came on his mind because his mouth opened just a little and remain open.

"What happened? Where are you going?" Asked Sheena.

Vivek turned his back right away on the question of Sheena and came quickly to her. "Maybe....maybe we can find that place."

Nikhil little surprised by this. "How?" He asked. Vivek immediately opened Google page on his mobile and searched the map of Chhattisgarh.

He opened a picture of it, black dots were pointed in the name of all districts of the state. The picture was the same as Vivek just seen on the poster. Vivek placed the page next to the picture on the mobile screen on the scrap car's bonnet and turned the page. On the backside of the page encircled a round with the pen and wrote Korba.

"Our journey began from here...with the first murder, then we came to Bilaspur." Vivek said. While looking at the map, He made an oblique line down to Korba in the left direction, marking a point on it and wrote Bilaspur, circled it. Then keeping a finger on the place from Bilaspur, aligned properly on the right, he said. "Then we came here in Champa." Pointing Champa with the pen, Vivek dragged a streak from the point of Bilaspur and joined them both together.

"Now the next one will be the district Raigarh, Bemetara, Baloda Baazaar, Bilaspur or Chhattisgarh's capital 'Raipur'. Bilaspur is not because we have come from there." Said Amit.

"Yes! Because if it was, then he had done that earlier." Vivek said.

Vivek pulled back the pen sandwiched between

his lips and marked another black point on that page. “The next target .... would be here.” Vivek said.

All eyes immediately went on the page. Vivek just made a black circle in which he wrote Baloda Bazaar.

Vivek said. “These people settled themselves very smartly. In their team, one is from North, one from the south, one from East and one from West. No one could not imagine that they all will place themselves here.” All of them understood the point of Vivek.

“I don’t know how Raghav knows all these places.” Sheena said.

Nikhil was listening to them quietly till now. He said, breaking his silence. “Vivek we cannot take the risk. How can you say?...”

Vivek cut the matter of Nikhil and said. “Be-cause of the pattern of the locations.” He made an oblique line from Champa to left side and added to Baloda Bazaar.

To see that specific shape on the map, Sheena said. “It is looking like ‘S’.”

“Yes! This is the logo of their lab. They have made locations on the points of this letter.” Vivek made it clear.

Nikhil’s face was showing expressions of panic which he was barely concealed. He said. “But Vivek!

Friend! We cannot take the risk. Because...because this is our last chance. If...if you have this theory wrong then we will lose the last member as well as Raghav.” Nikhil, daunting them this time, while talking with his back turned to them so that no one could suspect him by seeing his panicked face.

"I can understand your condition Nikhil! We have been unsuccessful so far. However, we can still catch him and the real mastermind and get them punished." Vivek, giving empathy to Nikhil, reached to him. He was not ready to give up. He explaining stretched out his hand to keep a hand on Nikhil's shoul-der. Nikhil was sensing that Vivek's voice was coming nearer, he instantly moved toward the vehicle. Vivek was so close to putting his hand on Nikhil's shoulder.

He opened the door of the vehicle and said them to all, allowing his back to them. "Okay! We took risks from starting then let's take last one too. We will see whatever happens. Come!"

So close. Nikhil blew out a breath.

Chapter eighteen

The last one

* * *

Time : Night 7:30 pm.

Vivek asked Amit the answer of a question which was bothering him. "Tell me something," Amit observing Vivek, responded and then looked on the front. "Who was that boy whom you were reprimanding in the studio?"

"That was Nitin! A very dangerous hacker. His act is nothing but short of magic. From ten-year-old, he took a firm grip on the computer." Amit said. "The day I caught him, then let him go on the condition that he would leave the job. Now he studies as well as helps his father in his shop."

"Oh! I guess I was barking up the wrong tree." Vivek saw Amit and said.

"Never mind. Forget about that now." Amit distracted his attention. "Once he did an amazing thing."

"What did he do?"

Here at the other side Amit and Vivek were conversing, Nikhil was looking for a chance to give Raghav a wake-up call. Sheena was quite close to him, therefore, he was compelled not to. Nikhil by calling spotted out that place in Baloda Baazaar where the Swachh Bharat Abhiyaan program was to be held.

"Come on!" After speaking on a call Nikhil called everyone.

"That deed was literally awesome." Vivek said about that hacker boy and moved ahead.

They first took Vivek's Scorpio from the complex and then vehicles ran towards that place. They were supposed to arrive within a few hours or maybe even sooner because they were going faster. Amit conveying situation to the police there, explained them the face of Raghav. They were under strict orders to arrest anyone who looks like that.

Amit was driving. Dissolving extended comfort there, he said to Nikhil. "The good thing is, he is defiantly moving in the same appearance till now. I have told officers his description. They'll catch him on sight."

"Hmmm!" Nikhil responded. Amit gave him a look and then looked towards the front again.

Raghav escaped from him, that might have become quite frustrating. Unaware of the Nikhil's true intentions, Amit pondered.

Vivek hit the bull's eye. Raghav is arriving there. Have to do something. Nikhil's focus was on making a success to the next step of his plan. He pulled his mobile. Amit's attention was on the road. Nikhil got a perfect opportunity to alert Raghav.

'Change the get up' Nikhil typed and sent to Raghav.

Amit's eye fell on the Nikhil same time. "Who is that sir?"

Nikhil smiled a little and said. "Payal! Only she can bother me in such situation."

On the other side, Vivek and Sheena sat quietly. They never sat silently so long. Vivek could see her through the mirror. He perceived her worry and love behind that silence. Sheena still did not want Vivek to be engaged in all this. Vivek did not want to hurt her. But he was helpless.

Both of their eyes met each other, for a moment, in front of the mirror. The next moment, Vivek concentrated on the road again there are something going on Sheena's mind. As Nikhil, Vivek didn't know true intentions of Sheena too and about her connections with Shivraam Dharmatma.

Time: Night 8:50 pm. Baloda Bazaar.

They reached their destination. There was a large ground called 'Dashehara Maidan' in front of them. People were sitting on chairs inside and enjoying the program. Some of the local leaders and legislators were sitting at the front of the queue. Two rows from behind were full of them. 'Mango people', the public were seated on rest of the chairs behind. For the promotion of sanitation, an act was playing based on the same theme on the stage. There was a huge crowd. Loud sounds of applause were indicating their enjoyment. Advertising campaigns were mounted in the perimeter of the field.

Vivek and the team had already taken stock of

the situation a bit far from there.

"I heard that this town has several tourist places like Sirpur, Turturia, Giroudpuri, Siddheswar Mandir and much more. I Thought whenever I would come here, will definitely visit those places. But situations aren't looking in my favor." Amit said looking around.

They were off the vehicles.

"I have come here many times to visit tourist places." Said Vivek.

"You saw that same." Said Sheena, looking at the start of the main arena.

The banner was mounted on up. In the same way the banner "Swachh Bharat Abhiyaan" was written as Vivek was drawn on his sketch. 'Swachh Bharat' in large fonts and the 'Abhiyaan' in small fonts on the downside.

"Sir!" A sub inspector and two constables arrived there. They went to them and stood in salute.

Nikhil asked to one. "What's the news?"

"Sir, the face description you told, no one got recognized like that neither heard out about any murder." He answered.

"That means still have hope for remaining alive of the last member." Amit said.

"Absolutely." Said Nikhil.

"What is the name of the next?" Sheena asked.

Vivek replied, "Dr. Akram Tripathi." He had his picture appeared on the mobile screen.

"Give them a photo and they will find him. It is possible that to present him here." Amit gave a suggestion.

Nikhil did some thinking. Amit and Vivek were about to act when they were stopped by Nikhil and he said. "Let's divide into two teams. Amit along with you and I'll keep Sheena with me. Her protection is needed the most."

Vivek looked at Sheena. She did not seem to agree with this suggestion. Vivek said holding her hand. "Nikhil is right."

"But," Sheena wanted to convince him but Vivek stopped her by holding her hands. Nikhil gestured him to move forward. The ground was full of crowd. The two team, with policemen there, took the each direction. Nikhil and Sheena went towards the right. Vivek and Amit took the left direction.

Amit and Vivek were palpating doctor in the crowd. Looking for the doctor in the queue, Vivek's eyes fell on Sheena. Even after being away, he could read her expressions.

"Oh no!!" Involuntarily came out of the Vivek's mouth. Surprise and fear broaden to his eyes.

"What happened?" Said Amit.

Vivek was so startled by the scene in front of him that he didn't respond, Amit's question remained unheard. Amit had not received a response, he looked that direction where Vivek was looking at.

"This is Raghav." Amit also fell in wonder.

Raghav now, had just gone behind Sheena. He was wearing a hat that covered the frontest part of his face. Black -clothing was replaced by a green T shirt. Blue jeans below. His same bag was hanging behind on his back.

Raghav had changed his appearance a little. Amit and Vivek did not take long to understand why the police did not find him yet.

Amit said, "Now it's confirmed Dr. Akram is here."

As the moment both overcame these moments of surprise, he was gone from Nikhil and Sheena.

"He is going towards the crowd." Said Amit and immediately put Nikhil on the phone. Vivek maintained his eyes completely on Raghav.

"Why sir is not receiving my call? Maybe because of the program they cannot hear the voice."

"Oh good. I found doctor Akram."

"Where?"

He pointed a finger and told Amit. "Look at that. He is only a short distance from Raghav." Amit saw doctor Akram. He was surprised a little bit to see the doctor. "Strange! He has not changed his phiz. But why?" Vivek said.

"It is not the time to think, you must stop Raghav from reaching him." Amit pulled out his gun and said . "This time let him taste his own medicine." He brought the gun back and saving from sights of others, fired two rounds down on the ground.

Hearing the gunfire nobody cared about the 'campaign' nor 'sanita-tion' they lifted their stuck butts from chairs and began to ran like hell.

Vivek saw Nikhil grabbing Sheena's hand and running to one direction, therefore, he was assured by his side.

"You hold Doctor. I'll help sir to catch Raghav." So saying, Amit ran towards Raghav and gestured the other officers to reach the same side. Doctors were also running but Vivek did not lose sight of him.

Vivek went in the middle of the crowd approached the doctor, holding his hand and began to take him with himself. "Come with me. This way."

"Who are you? Where are you taking me?" The doctor said, twitching his hand back.

Vivek again firmly grabbed his hand and pulled forcefully aside carrying said. "There is no time to explain, sir, trust me."

The doctor went with him because he was taking him the same direction where all people were fleeing. He also did not have a choice.

As they were fleeing, and slowly began to cross lanes - slowly people began to slow down. They arrived in a deserted area of the parish.

Vivek came running by clutching Doctor. Vivek stopped after coming here. The doctor stopped and began to stare in wonder at Vivek. After leaving his hand, he began painting by laying his hands on the knees.

"What is...Huff...all?" The doctor also questioned panting.

"I'll tell." Vivek said gasping.

Chapter nineteen

The shocking truth

* * *

Time : Night 9:10 pm .

They had been standing there almost for five minutes. Vivek had told the news of the death of the remaining members to Dr. Akram. He was in shock. He probably did not see any news that day. Vivek encouraged him to tell the whole thing. Doctor Akram told Vivek about the whole plan of their guide and mentor Shivraam Dharmatma. He told Vivek the whole thing from the death of Rama Tandon to gathering members and sending all to the new address.

"What was special in that stone?" Asked Vivek after hearing all.

"The stone had very high level of explosives. The biggest bomb could be made with its ten-gram weight fragments. An enemy knew about that and they wanted it at any cost." Doctor Akram was engaged in telling him the whole thing. Vivek went behind doctor, ambling. He was listening to him and also searching something on side of the road. His eyes stopped at an outdated shop on the front.

"We did this all for the country's sake but still Raghav seemed to be able to kill all of us. He will kill me too." The doctor was too lost in his words that he did not even look back. Vivek took out his copy from the pocket behind, opened it and started to make some-thing again by keeping it on the bonnet of a car parked ahead. It took some twenty seconds to make the picture complete.

Vivek picked up a stanchion lying down on the roadside after the picture's completion. It was shorter, stronger and slightly thicker. Vivek slowly moved forward towards the doctor. The doctor turned behind while talking. "But tell me, how did you people know about ..... aah !" Vivek hit on doctor's stomach with the stanchion, he screamed. He bowed down to the upper part. He did one more strenuous hit on the back. The doctor completely fell on the road. Vivek injured his legs badly by hitting there continuously.

"AAh!! What are you doing? Have you gone mad?" Doctor vociferously said in pain.

"So that you can not run." Vivek stopped hitting him. He put the stanchion on the bonnet of the car behind. The doctor was sore. Vivek said bringing a copy to him. "What are you doing here with him?" Asked Vivek showing him the sketch he just made.

The doctor suffering from pain, Replied. "You're hitting me becau...because of that...that picture?"

With angry red eyes, Vivek brought his face in front of doctor's face and said. "I told you the whole thing but didn't mention the killer's name." So hearing this, Doctor's eyes got overgrow.

While running with the doctor, grabbing his hand, Vivek had read his mind. He made two people's sketch on a copy. A man with curly hair on the head and french cut beard on the face, sweater on the top and wearing pants below. This description was matching perfectly with doctor Akram. He was shaking one hand and with another hand, he was handing suitcase over to another man whose appearance was perfectly matching with Raghav.

"You...you are having any misunderstanding." The doctor tried to give an explanation one more time and at the same time Vivek lifted up that stanchion to hit him again. Doctor shouted. "I'm telling, I'm telling!" Vivek calmed down loosening his grip on the stanchion.

"I am...I am the one who gave him the contract to kill Rama, I deal with the enemies of that stone and my nephew was with me in all this. I saw Rama taking all the data and stone before I got back from the lab. But I had not seen him giving it back. That's the mistake I made and then everything went wrong."

"It means you're the one four three, but if you're not the fourth target, then who is?" Vivek asked.

"The one who has the stone."

"That means Shivraam Dharmatma."

"No!" Doctor said. "Two days ago, the old disease took his life, but four days ago, he gave the stone to a trustworthy student. I did not even know about it until today. But a boy who used to work with him just sent a photo of the student. He was sold with great difficulty. While I was coming here running with you I sent that photo to Raghav, hiding from you."

"Raghav got all data?"

"Yes! I knew where they keep their important things, I had told that detail to Raghav."

"You guys met secretly. If you want you could kill

all of them one by one very Easily. Why didn't you do that?"

"No! First, even if I killed anyone of them until I could find another one they would have changed their address. Second, Dr. Sivraam was keeping an eye on all of us. So to assure them I and my nephew remained quiet. After we learned about his death, we three had a good chance and an only way to find their hideouts and kill them all four in just one day. But with the clues, we could barely find Sumit's location."

Startled Vivek. "One minute! If you did not know all of their hideouts then how did Raghav succeed in killing all of them?"

"Hahaha hahaha hahaha!!" Hearing the question, Akram's pain and fear evaporated. He started putting a slant laughter. He kept laughing, pointing his finger to Vivek. Vivek realized that Dr. was laughing on him. With his laugh, Vivek's anger grew. He further strengthened his grip on the stanchion to know more. But before he could hit doctor Akram he heard the sound of firing.

"Aah!!" screamed out, Akram. A bullet just penetrated his chest. Vivek immediately turned back towards the source of the sound of the shot, after turning, he saw above the roof of an old house.

"Raghav!" said Vivek, gun in hand, looking at the person standing on the deck. He ran away from there. Vivek couldn't do anything but stand there and watch him run. Raghav was far from his reach now.

Raghav arrived a while ago preventing himself from the police. Doctor's old body was not able to tolerate the strong stanchions. He had spat out his black truth in front of Vivek. Possibilities were there that Akram would have told him about Nikhil too. But to keep Nikhil's name in dark, Raghav killed doctor Akram.

Vivek immediately handled doctor Akram.

"Doctor! Doctor!" He shouted.

The doctor now could die anytime. He pulled his cell phone out from his pocket with his doddering hand and in broken - Tunes he said his last words to Vivek. "Save...save it..." The doctor died in front of him.

Vivek took the mobile. "Shit! It is having the pattern lock." Vivek said seeing the mobile screen. He cooled down his mind for few second, thinking of something. Then he put mobile into sleep mode. Now he could see the imprint of fingers on the screen of the doctor's mobile which was printed due to opening several times. An 'A' was made. He rotated his thumb the same way. "Thankfully, there was not a winding pattern." After opening the mobile lock Vivek spoke out in relief.

Vivek started the mobile filtrate. Mobile was empty completely. No numbers and no messages. Vivek then checked WhatsApp, he found a number in which a photo was sent. Vivek opened it and saw. Looking at the person in the picture his eyes torn from fear and surprise.

Vivek immediately ran fast. He called Nikhil, running.

Nikhil picked up the phone and said. "Hello!" Vivek said coming straight to the point immediately. "Save Sheena! She's the last target."

Chapter twenty

Trapped

❄ ❄ ❄

Time: 9.40 pm.

When Nikhil first heard about the Sheena being the fourth member from Vivek he couldn't believe his ears. He felt cheated. She was there with them the whole time and he was looking for her. That time Amit was with them because of that Nikhil was unable to do anything. But his mind was now engaged in weaving a new scheme so that he could separate her from the team.

Shortly after this, Vivek appeared running. Even after reaching there, Vivek was unable to control his speed. He was about to bump into Nikhil but before it could happen Nikhil held him instantly and made him sit on the chair placed there. He got very tired. He was looking at Sheena, gasping and asking many questions by his facial expressions. Sheena was still silent. She was also looking at Vivek. Vivek watched her long enough and kept gasping.

So after he ended his gasping, Sheena tried to say something. "Vivek I," Vivek kept his hand forward and stopped her from saying anything. He got up from his place and told her looking in the eye. “I do not know why did you conceal this fact from me, why put me in the dark. But at this point....saving your life is more important.”

Everyone wanted to know in detail what happened there, but all the things were left for later. It was necessary to protect Sheena at this hour.

Vivek came near Nikhil. Nikhil kept his distance. “Friend!! Now I have only trust on you.”

Nikhil was pleased inside and he assured Vivek. “Don’t you worry. I have an idea.”

“What?” Vivek said.

Before Vivek reached there, Nikhil had already finalized the plan. He explained his plan. “Raghav ran in this way, I’ll go to that way with Sheena. Here is a place in Outskirts where we can keep Sheena safe. I’ll take her there. You both distract Raghav.”

Listening to Nikhil’s plan, Vivek started thinking a bit when Amit erased his question by giving a heads up to the plan.

“That would be great” Amit said.

Sheena seemed to disagree with this plan. She did not want to leave Vivek. She said, expressing his opposition. “But I,” furthermore, even before she could say anything Vivek silenced her by grabbing her hand. He went to her. Nikhil and Amit got a bit off. Vivek said to Sheena holding her both hands. “ I’m not gonna let anything happen to you. Do not worry.”

Sheena looked helpless at this time. She agreed and embraced Vivek. She said. “Even I pretended to not know anything all this time but I really love you." As soon as she finished her talk she came to Nikhil and both headed to the vehicle.

****

Four days ago from today. January 2016. Maharashtra .

Just a short while ago, in the wooded area where Sheena came to meet somebody, in a car, was Shivraam Dharmatma. She was waiting for him to say something.

While he was silent, Sheena quickly observed the stuff on the table between them. There was a newspaper kept on the table. Seemed of the same day. A paperweight was there holding the other papers down. A transparent pot was placed near paper-weight with some bunches of flowers under it. A rose was one of them and along with it, there were two blue and yellow flowers more, which Sheena had no idea about. Apart from all this, her sight captured a little brown box which never put there.

"Things are exactly going like you said. Because of your teaching techniques I'm able to divert my attention to another thing whereby nothing came on my mind even by mistake and Vivek could not read anything from my mind. He didn't know that I know about his powers."

Shivraam responded. "Hmm!! Now the another important thing," well, He had become an old man of seventy-five years but his freshness and enthusiasm never let anyone feel that he was an old man. He was always a ball of fire. But today, his exhaustion and despair appeared from his face. Facial wrinkles were indicating some kind of defeat. Eyes were tipping not to sleep in relief. His body was feeling loose. His whole personality appeared to lack the enthusiasm that Sheena had ever seen before.

"Sir, if your condition...?" Sheena was about to stand from her place when doctor Shivraam's hand gestured to make her sit again. "You shouldn't come here in such a state. If I knew, I'll have never let you come." Sheena spoke in the concerned tone.

"Thought should meet you the same way I used to before going." Shivraam said. This time, his strong and weighty voice did not feel the same now. Now his age could be felt distinctly on his voice. "You know, how many jobs I didn't finish till date?" He asked the question.

She did not respond but kept looking at him silently. Shivraam, joining his thumb and index finger together, made a circle and answered himself. "Zero."

"Sir, you..."

He further said to Sheena interrupting. "My illness! Probably will kill me tomorrow. So I came here to tell you all the things that remain." He opened the box and pulled a shining stone from that. Detaches the rock to the side of the Sheena, Shivraam said. "You keep it."

Sheena looked familiar to the stone. She switched over to her Sir after seeing a glimpse of the stone, and said again. "How did I... I cannot take such a big responsibility."

"And I now can only trust you." The question emerges on Sheena's face.

"I was looking outside for my enemies till now, whereas from my investigation I came to know that someone from inside is compromising. Doubting outsiders I just wasted my time. I just wish I would have listened to you first then I had found out that traitor today. Now I only have to find his name and I will. But if I failed. I want you to finish it. You're the one who did the initial searching about the stone whereas even I didn't believe you. I now have only trust on your abilities. Nobody knows about you except me. Asif also first time saw you today. So keep this stone with you."

Sheena placed that stone in the boxes and pulled it to her side.

"That guy...Vivek.. Stay close to him. If that man's speech was true as Rama told me, then he could be the 'sixth sense or divine eye' person who he mentioned that night." Said Shivraam.

When Vivek told her the truth about his abilities, Sheena took it as a joke. But soon his activities made her think about it seriously. She knew about the prediction associated with the stone. She told Shivraam and he instructed her to become friends with Vivek. She found the truth very soon and told Shivraam.

"Being a scientist, you still believe in these type of things? Vivek meeting with me is a big co-incident nothing else. How could it be possible that the person referred on that prevailing prognostication about the stone, met me one day who is the daughter of your best friend and student as well."

"Coincidence," Shivraam first smiled listening to her and said further. "There is no such a thing as co-incidence. It is a time that decides everyone's part and puts them together in its own way. And anyway as a Scientist I could not turn my back on the possibilities." Sivaram added. "There are possibilities that he would engage and finish all this according to prediction."

"Sir, you do not worry...I will keep the stone safe. And about Vivek, I will not let anything happen to him. I'll take his death on my own if I have to. Because the closeness has become the reality which was started as drama." Said Sheena. Shivraam felt her care and love about Vivek in her voice. Vivek was now the apple of Sheena's eye.

Chapter twenty one

The biggest blow

❄ ❄ ❄

Now. Time : night 10:00 pm today.

"Sir Sivaram explored the rookie, was just a little bit closer. But two days later, life cheated him. Therefore I could not go with Vivek to meet his parents. As soon as I started the investigation from my side, their killing began. Now I'm realizing that why Shivraam sir choose Chhattisgarh to hide them. Because I live here. Thought I will catch that rookie and the murderer with the help of Vivek but I got concerned about him as well. I was being mean sometimes, therefore, I used to tell him to drop the case because as per that old man, people engaged with the stone, died. And all that happened, like how the scientist died because of the Akram and his nephew. Wonder who's that scoundrel?"

"You're gonna die too because of that scoundrel." Nikhil mulled.

Sheena was informing all details to Nikhil in the way. Nikhil continued his acting. He said convincing her. "Don't you worry. I'll catch that bastard and must bring before you."

Sheena smiled and said. "Thanks, Nikhil! You are a good friend. I am confident that you and Vivek together must catch him."

Here Raghav was also geared up. He had still hidden on a secluded street. He was waiting for the next message. His mobile vibrated. He pulled out his mobile. Nikhil's message was there.

'I have Sheena. Your fourth target.'

Raghav typed a message on his mobile to answer. Sheena was leisurely sitting there at the mercy of Nikhil. Raghav's message got delivered on Nikhil's mobile. Due to outskirts area, there was the slow internet connection, therefore, message's intercommunication service was the little bit slow.

Nikhil read the message in thoughts. 'Now what next?'

Nikhil began to write the message, keeping an eye on the road. It was an outer region, therefore this thing was not that big of a deal but hiding the messages from Sheena was. Soon he got to know that even this was not a problem because she was concerned for Vivek. Lying his elbow on the window while she was enjoying the cool breeze outside appeared as she was thinking. It made it easier for Nikhil.

He began to instruct Raghav by sending messages.'Hit the bypass road to Bilaspur.'

Raghav also driving a car was waiting for Nikhil's message. He saw the message.

Raghav was immediately swerved and further increased his speed. He carefully, paying attention to the road, sent next message. 'Taken.'

Here Raghav's message came to Nikhil. He saw the message.

"All are ready?" Amit, in front of the officers, said. Aside from all this, Amit and Vivek were engaged in their preparations.

Three police gypsies were in front of Amit. In every gypsy three officers Inspector, Sub-Inspector and Constable were there. "We have to catch a very dangerous contract killer. There should be no mistake. This is probably our last chance." Amit explained all.

Amit came to Vivek, raising his hand to his shoulder to encouraging him and said. "Do not worry! Nothing will happen to Sheena. This time surely Raghav will be caught." Head nodded, Vivek expressed his confidence in Amit in a peaceful way.

Here Sheena was getting away from their reach. Some six - seven minutes after driving,

Nikhil typed the next message. 'After ten kilometers you will see a first 'dhaba'. From there, take a right turn.'

Message delivered. Raghav saw the message and did as it written. Unaware of all this, she was still lost in thoughts of Vivek.

Nikhil, watching Sheena sent the next message. 'After a kilometer will appear a ground area, stop the vehicle. I'm coming towards the front.'

Raghav saw Nikhil's message. After while he stopped going forward. He looked up. This place was a deserted field. Stood down from the car and began to wait for Nikhil.

Taking another short-cut Nikhil also reached the destination.

"Reached." A few minutes later he said to Sheena.

They both landed from Nikhil's vehicle. "Where are we?" Sheena asked Nikhil. Nikhil did not respond.

Sheena looked ahead. Ticking off the bonnet of the car, in front of them, a man was standing.

"Raghav?" Recognizing the man, the name came from Sheena's mouth.

"Wow!" Nikhil, to correct his spectacles by moving it, came near to her and said. "You identified him even in the dark. Hats off to your eyes."

Astonished Sheena was looking at Nikhil. "Come on! Gimme this dangerous weapon!" Nikhil snatched the mobile from Sheena's hand and kept it.

Chapter twenty-two
Plan revealed

❄ ❄ ❄

Time : night 10:30 pm.

"You... You did all this? Raghav was your man?" Sheena asked. She was in a huge shock as she saw Nikhil was behind all this. Raghav was standing relaxed there with his gun out.

"Yes! I gave him contract him to kill those scientists. I am the bastard nephew of my maternal uncle Dr. Akram." Nikhil said, showing his crooked smile.

Sheena recovering herself from that shock said. "But.. but why and how did you do this all?"

"I don't think telling you is compulsory. But since you're gonna give me that stone, therefore, I'll tell you everything. It all started when my uncle told me the beauty of the stone. It was a treasure for me. My 'Mama' Dr. Akram and I deal in the billions with the enemies of the country and took the advance. Now I just had to grab the stone. I gave the contract to Raghav and sent him to Rama Tandon. First, he couldn't get the data but a huge mess happened."

"He killed Sir Rama and then after knowing

that, Sir Shivraam sent them all here."

"Correct! I must admit, the Old man's mind was amazing. My uncle and I freed the sweat to detect even one of them. But I also had to make money and save my life. And look! Where I found them, in my own State. Now not only I have all the data, thanx to Raghav, but also a guardian of Stone, you."

"But why did you engage us with you? Weren't we kind of a risk for you, especially Vivek?"

"Vivek! Danger!" He started laughing loudly. The laughing pattern was same as doctor Akram's. He came up to Sheena and said, stopping his laughter. "He is the one who helped me kill everyone."

"What the fuck are you talking?" Sheena's anger was growing even more. Nikhil's word was now working like putting fuel in the fire for Sheena. If she wasn't handcuffed in vehicle's front shield, then she would definitely strike him.

"Have you ever thought why Raghav always came out killing where we were about to reach. Why it never happened that we are going somewhere else and he escaped killing someone else?" On listening to this, her mind's layers started to unravel.

"You mean,"

"...That Vivek has the power but I am the one who was using it. You got that right. Vivek did not locate them, I made him." Sheena got stunned by his dialogue. These words seemed like hammers striking her brain.

"A week ago, the day I found out about it after that kidnapping incident, I began making plans. Remember that night when we first met at the restaurant? Later that night he told me about his power and also about his visiting and returning plans with his parents. From Raghav's seeking for the lift to till the end, everything was planned by me."

"How did you rely on Vivek this much that he will find out all locations?"

"Was not sure. I risked everything on Vivek and the fact that the members were dying, will give clues anyhow so that we could reach the next one. Anyway, if I had not finished, 'they' would have killed me. So I had to do something to save myself. And look at my luck, all bets were right. We barely found one in two months even he was in my town and through him, Vivek found rest of them just in one day. The perfect plan. It was very difficult to extract things from one's mouth but entering the mind was the little bit easy. I knew that Vivek was not going to do it easily, therefore, Raghav was killing them also to put pressure on Vivek to give his best so that he could save another one. After killing doctor David D'Souza, uncle had called the Raghav for a meeting here because we were going to find out about this stone's guardian student. Therefore, when Vivek touched Raghav, he sensed everything about the 'Swachh Bharat' program going on here."

"And that, you did not want to happen?"

"You are really a very intelligent girl. Coming to Baloda Bazaar with you all was not the part of my plan, therefore, I tried to not let that happen. But see! Coming here, even by mistake I found out about you and that poor Vivek served you on a plate to me."

"You were with us all the time, either with Vivek or Amit. Then how did you tell Raghav about the locations?"

Nikhil came near to her again, put a finger on her forehead and bringing it from her cheek to lips, said stopping it. "I was trying to convince my girlfriend 'Payal' the whole time, What do you think who was that?" He winked at her smiling. Sheena pounced on him but the prick of the handcuff reminded her of her being tied.

"What are you....you going to do with Vivek?" Sheena anxiously asked.

"The same thing I had to do unwillingly with the scientists because of their patriotism and skills. I had to sacrifice my maternal uncle too....I will miss Vivek."

Going to the Raghav, Nikhil looked back and said. "Enough of talks. Now we have to torture you because I know you're not going to give up the stone so easily Aaah! "

Nikhil was going forward, talking to Sheena by turning his head back because of which, he was unaware of the movements of Raghav, Who hit Nikhil hard on his forehead with a gun. Nikhil faltered and Raghav pulled out handcuff and tied Nikhil with It. He also took out his gun and kept it.

"Raghav! What...what the fuck," his hands were handcuffed, trying to twitch it when his eyes seen toward the front, the Earth slipped from his foot. "Nayak!!" Nikhil saw Amit behind Raghav. His eyes glided slightly more and they burst by a big surprise.

"V...Vivek!!" Nikhil said adding. Vivek and Sheena were standing there with Amit who was taking back Nikhil's gun from Raghav.

The next moment, the headlights burnt one by one around him. Nikhil rotated his eyes and found out that the whole ground was surrounded by police gypsies. All the officers were standing there in position to fire.

The table had turned.

Chapter twenty-three

The game changer

* * *

Nikhil had noticed red colored spots and scratches on Raghav's face indicating damages gifted by Amit for sure. Because he just gave Nikhil the same gift after tying him with handcuffs. Nikhil was now down on the ground puking blood from his mouth. Amit's legs and his boots also participated in this equally. Amit, for the sake of his friendship, gave a present to Vivek to hit Nikhil. Vivek's woodland shoes gave chance to Nikhil to taste its durability. Damaged face and focusing headlights were making his face more horrible. He was not even able to open his eyes due to the lights.

Vivek came near Nikhil, grabbed his hairs and pulled them up and said. "Thinking about how the hell, was it possible?" Said Vivek with showing his angry red eyes and pointed his finger to Raghav who was sitting on a gypsy.

After taking the gun from Raghav, Amit tied his hands with a handcuff.

"Raghav, there is also going crazy thinking

about all this." Vivek said in a satire but in a serious tone. "I'll tell you....by Magic. Let me take you half an hour ago, back to dashehra maidaan, after you left with Sheena."

Half an hour ago. Baloda Bazaar Dashehara ground. Time: 10.00 pm.

As per his new scheme, Nikhil just took Sheena with him. On that ground, Amit and Vivek, trusting Nikhil were about to go to catch Raghav.

"All are ready!" Amit front of the officers said. "We have to catch a very dangerous killer. There should be no mistake. This is probably our last chance." Amit explained all.

Amit came to Vivek and raised his hand to his shoulder to courage him and said. "Do not worry! Nothing will happen to Sheena. This time surely Raghav will be caught." Head nodded, Vivek expressed his confidence in Amit in a peaceful way. He seemed like thinking of something.

"Call Nitin, The hacker, fast." Amit going forward to the vehicle turned his head toward Vivek in the response to suddenly hearing his voice.

"What?... what are you?..." Amit said but Vivek interrupted him between and said. "No time for explanation. Just do it." His words were running like a runner. Vivek's expressions told him situation's gravity and Amit called. His phone was ringing, while Vivek showed Amit a picture which shocked him for a moment. Vivek just made that. His face was asking a question, Vivek understood and answered. “Later..”

Nitin received Amit’s call and connected him to Vivek. Vivek instructed him. “We have two numbers here which you have to hack and inform us the messages they are sending to each other.” Vivek told him that numbers and then everything started to happen like Horse-racing.

They put the phone on speaker. Nitin said. “Done. What next?”

“That first number I gave you, tell me what he is messaging” Said Vivek. He turned to Amit and spoke. “Now it’s our turn to play with them both.” Amit nodded his head.

‘I have Sheena. Your fourth target.’ Nitin pronounced.

This was the first message Nikhil sent to Raghav. Vivek closed his eyes for a moment and his father’s voice started humming on his mind again. Once his father prepared him for the situation like this.

“When life comes at the risk, people’s minds work in two ways. Either it starts to work fast or stop completely. I pray to God not to come that day in your life, but if it happens, you have to run your mind like a train.”

His love’s life was in danger. Instead of shutting off, his brain started running fast. He was familiar with Nitin’s hacking skills.

‘Hit the bypass road to Bilaspur.’ Read Nikhil’s next message.

Vivek instantly instructed Nitin. “Replace Bilaspur with Raipur.”

"Annnnnnd...done." Heard Nitin's voice with 'kit-kit' of the keyboard. So listening, Amit prepared all the gypsies. Following Amit's vehicle, all started going towards Raipur bypass.

"We have to change their timings also." Amit pointed out.

"Right." Vivek replied smiling.

After ten kilometers will show a first 'dhaba'. From there, take a right turn.' Nitin told them another one message from Nikhil's.

"Replace ten with four, 'dhaba' with hotel and right with left." Said Vivek.

"Annnnnd," 'kit-kit' again on the keyboard. "... did that too." Nitin told by expressing his ease.

Amit was in the driving seat as usual. Vivek was next to him had taken out his mobile, opened location option on the screen. He looked it carefully and said. "Sheena is exactly heading toward with Raghav where we want them to. It means our plan is working."

"It takes half an hour to reach where Nikhil was exactly calling him. But as per your changes, it'll take ten minutes to reach where we are calling him." Having knowledge about both routes was proving very useful now for Vivek.

"After a kilometer will appear a ground area, stop the vehicle. I'm coming from the front.' That was the last message from Nikhil's.

"Great." Sparks emerged on Vivek's face. "Stay with us." Vivek told to Nitin.

They all arrived there. Raghav reached there after two minutes. They all had doused their vehicle's headlights. After reaching him there, all lit up together. Before Raghav could understand anything or escape, the view around him had changed. The police force was standing before him pointing the gun to his head.

"You still have a gun in your hand and can shoot me, if you want to. But then all of them will shoot you. Don't worry they're not going to encounter. They will target on your both hands and legs and will make you handicapped for rest of your life. But if you do whatever we say, you can live your life restfully in jail."

After being quiet for a moment, Amit said further. "Now you decide. And please..don't take longer than two seconds. You see, we have time criteria here." This was the old way of Amit's when it's hard to tell that whether is it torture or meekness.

Raghav was forced. He dropped his gun.

Amit came to him and welcomed with some quick kicks and punches. After that quick action, he took him in the gypsy and they quickly reached the place where Nikhil was diverted to by taking another shortcut and did the same, switching down headlights and waiting for Nikhil, thing.

Now.

Nikhil's torn eyes were staring at him. Vivek just told him about complete details of his coup. He still did not want to believe in the view.

Amit said. "My grandpa used to say that if you are not succeeding after hard work then you must know that someone from inside is causing a mess. Because outside hindrance is to make you stronger it's insiders who make voids. Today I'm watching that line becoming reality."

"You...you how.. all." Added Nikhil was not even able to say words correctly.

Vivek replied. "We believed that you are doing this whole thing with Raghav through mobile messages. Because through calling, it would be difficult and we didn't see you talking over the phone. I got Raghav's number through your uncle and we already had your number. We were tracking you two through the location app too."

"How? How did you find my truth?" Nikhil handled himself somehow and asked.

Vivek took out a page from his jean's back pocket and showed him a page. "This is the picture which ... In which my uncle and Raghav are dealing. Then," Nikhil could say anything further before, Vivek opened a little bit of the page which was directed towards the rear. This was the same picture which he made after reading Doctor Akram's mind but with less truth. Now it was the whole picture. Nikhil had stood behind his uncle.

"I saw this complete vision when you come in contact."

"But...but I didn't give you any chance to came in contact with me? Then how?"

Vivek came and spoke softly in his little voice. "Do you remember you had asked me that, minimum how long it takes to be in contact to read someone's mind." Nikhil was listening to wonder. Vivek added. "When I came running to tell you about Doctor Akram then,"

"This ... It can not be. I,"

"You stopped me holding with your hands... that's one." Vivek showed his finger. "Immediately made me sit...that's two." He showed the second finger. "And as long as the hand removed.." Vivek showed the third finger.

"Three!! Three seconds?" The last thing Nikhil completed.

Putting down back the ring finger and the index finger, completing matter. "And these three seconds finished you and your game." Now there was only 'middle finger' of Vivek in opposite to Nikhil's eyes.

"Whatever you confess here was sent to com-missioner sir. You're finished." Amit came forward and said showing him his mobile, shaking, opened recording option. "We not doubting you, was your greatest strength, but as soon as we knew about you, it becomes your biggest weakness."

"You will not be blown as much as I when I heard from your mouth that in the death of the greatest scientists, I was the one who was responsible. I wish...I wish I would have excused for one murder." Vivek said. Blood came into his eyes were proof of the truth of every word. Nikhil was still looking at Vivek with eyes torn.

Amit signaled to move Nikhil. A sub - inspector was pulling away Nikhil.

He went with him forward and suddenly started murmuring something. "It.. It can not happen. I can not lose." Nikhil's mental balance was shaken. "I can not lose." He forgot everything and vociferously took the officer's gun and turned to shoot, shouting at Vivek. Sheena and Vivek surprised by his scream.

Dhany ! Dhany ! Dhany ! Shot three bul-lets. Sheena looking at the view, became a statue. There were three holes in the Nikhil's chest. The blood was coming out from there. Sheena rotated her eyes and saw that smoke was flying out of the Amit's gun which was pointed toward Nikhil's. Amit once again saved the life of Vivek's. Amit's promptness to Nikhil once again worked here.

Sheena ran and hugged Vivek. Vivek also felt that moment of death terribly. He sighed with relief and expressed his gratitude by watching Amit. Amit also shook his head and replied, lead to the body of Nikhil.

Amit bowed and closed the eyes of Nikhil's corpse and said. " I never told you, but I did not like you." Amit called the ambulance and the police started taking Raghav to prison.

Amit came to Vivek and Sheena, said. "Let's go."

"One minute." Sheena preventing both from going and said to Vivek, separating herself from his chest. Suddenly her expression changed and she angrily began to blow punches on his arms in girly style. "What a deadly plan, if your plan had messed up even a little bit I would be taking a selfie with God now."

"Hey! Hey! Hey! We kept track of your location via the Internet." Vivek said in his defense, hearing that Sheena calmed down and naively started to fix Vivek's jacket.

Chapter twenty four
Unfinished business

* * *

Next day. Morning. Location: Champa.

It was morning. The event took place on the inside of the Muskan studio terrorized all but life did not stop, nor stayed in Krishna Complex. All the fear and sorrow in the heart took their daily tasks. Vivek, Sheena, and Amit had been standing outside the complex.

"Nitin!" Amit made a sound. Nitin hanging a bag on the back was entering into the complex. He looked back, hearing the sound. "Come here!" Amit called him.

Seeing Amit, Nitin's mood got spoiled. "What? Do you want to do that message dance again with someone?" He said, making a tight voice.

"Message-Dance?" Sheena asked curiously. "Yes! Yesterday, what he did to Nikhil and Raghav, he calls it message-dance and he specialize in that." Vivek said. "Ohh!" Said Sheena.

Luckily Vivek had asked Amit about Nitin's quality. Nitin himself was unaware that he's going to solve a big trouble. The important thing for him was just to obey Amit's instructions so that he wouldn't tell his dad about his deed and spending one night in jail. Sheena opened the front door of the parked Scorpio behind. Nitin was peeking curiously.

Sheena pulled a bag from inside, said. "The favor you did last night on us, we can't pay it back but please accept this small gift as a thank you." Sheena handed him the bag. Nitin, seen opening the bag. In it, was brand new and an expensive laptop. Nitin was jubilant. "That does not mean the next time you've got the freedom to do it." Amit interrupted his joy by saying. "...Until I say so."

Nitin whispered. "Bitter gourd."

"Did you say something?" Going back Amit, turned and Nitin replied. "No!!.. Your ears are ringing." Vivek and Sheena smiled.

"The one thing we couldn't find out was, what does One Four Three stands for? Why Raghav called them that? Nikhil told him to call that." Suddenly struck Amit's mind, said to Vivek.

"Me neither." Replied Vivek. Sheena shrugged and said. "Neither do I, But as we all know that it indicates 'I love you.'"

"And that's a virus for computer systems." Nitin answered, as soon as he heard. He was going but hadn't reached far enough. They all looked at him with surprise on their faces. "Believe me, I'm a hacker. 'I love you' is one of the most dangerous virus." Nitin added.

His answer explained all.

"We were the system and Nikhil was the virus for us. And same applied for the scientist's group. Akram was the virus for the group." Vivek said.

Then they sat in the vehicles and went back towards their paths.

Sheena was driving this time whereas Vivek was silent. Even though they overcame a big trouble but he was looking heavyhearted. Sheena sensed that feeling.

He said. "I wish I could save the scientists."

It was very crucial that Sheena pulls him out from his failure guilt. She stopped the Scorpio on the side of the road and said. "It was not your fault you know that, right? You had been used. So don't cry over split milk. And I know this is not enough but Shivraam sir already arranged the insurance for their families as future security and I must tell you that prophecy was correct."

"How?"

"You did break the queue by saving me." "Hmmm... Yesterday, that two masterminds made us dance." Vivek said to Sheena.

"Two not three. You were the third one who finally made them dance." Sheena looked at him and said. Vivek smiled at this point. Seeing him smile, Sheena took a sigh of relief.

"Tell me one thing?"

"Ask?" Sheena replied.

"How did you manage to not to think about all this stuff when you had been with me?" Asked the question which he couldn't ask last night.

"Shivraam sir taught me to neutral the mind. But the second most helping thing was...."

"Was??"

She grabbed his hand very affectionately and said."...Your love. I used to get lost with you in the moments." She said and they shared a love moment.

About the Author

* * *

Ashutosh Singh Rajput is a civil engineer, studied from Bhilai Institute Of Technology, Raipur, Chhattisgarh.

He was born and lives in Korba, Chhattisgarh.

He loves reading fictional/ fantasy stories, specially comic books. His reading habits since childhood helped him in increasing his reading skills. He believes this is the reason which gave him the writing skills too.

Even at this age he loves reading comics and watching superhero movies and T.V series.

Apart from this novel, he has also written a few comic book stories for comic companies.

He chose to became an author because he knew that he could become a better writer/author than an engineer. His degree surely says that he is an engineer but he is a writer at heart.

He loves listening to music too. He believe music keeps him alive and rejuvenated.

He is a strong believer of Lord Krishna and his principles.

Email id: ashutoshsinghr8@gmail.com